"Give me a month," she said, "and I'll change your mind about dismantling Lassiter's assets."

Interesting. "So you think I'll win this takeover battle?"

Becca lifted her chin. "Four weeks."

"One day."

"One week."

"On one condition."

"Name it."

What the hell. "I'd rather show you."

He slid a hand around her waist and drew her in as his mouth dropped over hers.

* * *

Taming the Takeover Tycoon is a
Dynasties: The Lassiters novel—

A Wyoming legacy of love, lies and redemption!

* * *

If you're on Twitter,
tell us what you think of Harlequin Desire!
#harlequindesire

Dear Reader,

When Wyoming billionaire J. D. Lassiter passed away unexpectedly, bereft family members and associates were left shaking their heads. Angelica was J.D.'s favorite—his *princess*. So why was his only daughter (and acting head of Lassiter Media) all but snubbed in her beloved father's will? Corporate raider Jack Reed says his late friend J.D. wasn't thinking straight. Furthermore, he has offered to help Angelica mount a takeover bid to regain control of the company that is rightfully hers.

Coordinator of the Lassiters' Charity Foundation Becca Stevens admired J.D. There must be *some* good reason controlling interest was left to Angelica's ex-fiancé. Meanwhile, rumors are rife, shares are down and public support for the foundation is circling the drain. Before the family destroys itself, and all the good the foundation does along with it, Becca must make Jack Reed reconsider— back down, move on—*or else*.

The toughest wars are waged over the concept of good versus evil. In this installment of Dynasties: The Lassiters, Becca and Jack are not only worthy opponents on the business battlefield, their sexual chemistry is downright dangerous.

I hope you enjoy *Taming the Takeover Tycoon!*

Best wishes,

Robyn

www.robyngrady.com

@robyngrady on Twitter

TAMING THE
TAKEOVER TYCOON

—

ROBYN GRADY

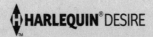

Special thanks and acknowledgment are given to Robyn Grady for her contribution to the Dynasties: The Lassiters miniseries.

Recycling programs
for this product may
not exist in your area.

ISBN-13: 978-0-373-73331-6

TAMING THE TAKEOVER TYCOON

Printed in U.S.A.

www.Harlequin.com

Books by Robyn Grady

Harlequin Desire

The Billionaire's Bedside Manner #2093
Millionaire Playboy, Maverick Heiress #2114
Strictly Temporary #2169
Losing Control #2189
A Wedding She'll Never Forget #2216
Temptation on His Terms #2243
One Night, Second Chance #2292
Taming the Takeover Tycoon #2318

Silhouette Desire

The Magnate's Marriage Demand #1842
For Blackmail...or Pleasure #1860
Baby Bequest #1908
Bedded by Blackmail #1950
The Billionaire's Fake Engagement #1968
Bargaining for Baby #2015
Amnesiac Ex, Unforgettable Vows #2063

*The Hunter Pact

Other titles by this author available in ebook format.

ROBYN GRADY

was first contracted by Harlequin in 2006. Her books feature regularly on bestsellers lists and at award ceremonies, including the National Readers' Choice Awards, the Booksellers' Best Awards, CataRomance Reviewers' Choice Awards and Australia's prestigious Romantic Book of the Year.

Robyn lives on Australia's gorgeous Sunshine Coast, where she met and married her real-life hero. When she's not tapping out her next story, she enjoys the challenges of raising three very different daughters, going to the theater, reading on the beach and dreaming about bumping into Stephen King during a month-long Mediterranean cruise.

Robyn knows that writing romance is the best job on the planet and she loves to hear from her readers! You can keep up with news on her latest releases at www.robyngrady.com.

For Penny and Gracie,
Two very cool ladies.
xoxo

One

The Robin Hoods of this world were Becca's heroes. As she watched Jack Reed strike a noble pose then draw back and release an arrow that hit dead center of his target, the irony wasn't lost on her.

Jack Reed was no Robin Hood. He was anathema to everything she stood for. To every living, breathing thing she believed in. Beyond all else, people ought to give back—even sacrifice—to support others who need help. Some mistook that level of compassion for weakness, but Becca was far from easy prey.

Looking *GQ*-hot in jeans and a white button-down, cuffs folded back on strong forearms, Reed lowered the bow and focused on his guest. The slant of his mouth was so subtle and self-assured, Becca's palm itched to slap the smirk off his face. She might have done it, too, if she thought it'd shake him up some. But it was said displays of true emotion only amused him.

Jack Reed owned a property in his hometown of Cheyenne, Wyoming, as well as two residences here in L.A.: an ultramodern penthouse apartment in a downtown high-rise building that he'd purchased as well as this spectacular Beverly Hills estate. With a quiver slung across his broad back, he sauntered over the manicured lawn to meet her. Although he was expecting her visit, Becca doubted he would welcome what she had to say.

She introduced herself. "Becca Stevens, director of the Lassiter Charity Foundation." She nodded at the target. "A perfect bull's-eye. Well done."

"I took up archery in college," he said in a voice so deep and darkly honeyed, the tone was almost hypnotic. "I try to squeeze some practice in every week."

"Difficult with your schedule, I imagine." All that dismantling of companies and banking the proceeds had to take up oodles of time. "I appreciate you seeing me."

His smile, designed to disarm, got bigger. "Any friend of J.D.'s is a friend of mine."

"If J. D. Lassiter were alive, he might not count *you* as a friend at the moment."

The smile widened more. "Straight for the jugular, Ms. Stevens?"

Given Jack Reed was a highly successful corporate raider, he ought to be used to the approach. "I thought you'd appreciate it."

"I only want to help Angelica Lassiter reclaim what she rightly deserves."

Becca let out a humorless laugh and then sighed. "Ah, sorry. Just the idea of someone like you being in any way self-sacrificing..."

His gaze sharpened. "Angelica was J.D.'s only child."

"You're forgetting Sage and Dylan."

"They are Ellie Lassiter's orphaned nephews, adopted after J.D. and Ellie had been told by doctors—"

"I know the background, Jack."

"Then you'll also know that Angelica, J.D.'s own flesh and blood, was his favorite—that he'd entrusted her with the running of Lassiter Media those crucial months before his death. It makes no sense that his will should insult her with a paltry ten percent while controlling voting interest of J.D.'s multibillion-dollar company goes to Angelica's ex-fiancé—" Jack paused for effect "—even if J.D. had handpicked Evan McCain for his daughter."

"J.D. might have liked Evan for a son-in-law. No one would argue he has remarkable business sense." Becca joined Jack as he headed off toward his target. "But Angelica trusted Evan. They fell in love."

"Betrayed by the man she was ready to marry. Tragic, wouldn't you say?"

Oh, please. "Evan had nothing to do with J.D.'s will."

"Maybe. Maybe not. But nothing stops him from reinstating to Angelica what should be hers now. He could do the decent thing by the woman he professes to love." Jack's lips twitched. "I don't know how he sleeps at night."

An image flashed into Becca's mind—Jack Reed lying butt naked on a rumpled sheet, fingers thatched behind his head, an unmistakable thirst reflecting in the depths of his glittering onyx eyes. Nerve endings ignited and flashed over her skin. The tingle raced through to her core, all the way down to her toes.

Reed was an attractive man; she would go so far as to say he was exceptional. If half of what the tabloids published was true, hoards of women had surrendered to the drugging heat she felt radiating off him now. The effect was gripping—beguiling—and, in Becca's case, about as welcome as boiling water on a third-degree burn.

As they continued to walk, she tried to stay focused.

"I'm here to implore you, in J.D.'s memory, to show some human decency. Walk away from this. After her father's death, Angelica's in no shape to link arms with the likes of you."

"Don't underestimate Angelica." His classically chiseled profile hardened as his chin lifted a notch. "She's stronger than you think."

"Right now, she's desperate."

He laughed, a somehow soothing and yet cynical sound. "You don't beat around the bush, do you, Becca?"

No time. "You own an interest in Lassiter Media and rumors are rife. People are bracing for a hostile takeover bid. The charity's donations are down. Regular beneficiaries are actually looking at other options. Want to guess why?"

"I'm sure you'll tell me."

Damn right she would. "The name Jack Reed means trouble—the kind of trouble clear-minded people run a mile to avoid."

He blinked slowly and grinned as if the description was something to savor. "As long as Angelica wants my help, I'll give it."

"You sought her out," she reminded him, "not the other way around."

"Your point?"

Her heart was pounding in her ears. No one wanted to make an enemy of this man, but Becca had a principle to defend. A fight to win. Hell, she'd faced worse situations than this and survived.

"I know what you're up to," she said as they neared the target, "even if Angelica can't or won't face the truth. After you've used her to gain majority control over Lassiter Media interests, you'll aim the next arrow at her back. You'll sell off Lassiter assets like you have with every other company you've acquired."

"Got it. I wear the black hat."

"Simple, isn't it?"

"If only."

Lord above, how she wanted to shake this man. "Seriously, how much money does one person need? Is this worth betraying your friend's memory? J.D.'s family?"

"This is not about money."

"With you, it's always about money."

His jaw flexed as he stopped in front of the target and freed the arrow.

"I understand your desire to help, but Angelica and I have this covered. And make no mistake." His uncompromising gaze pierced hers. "We intend to win."

Becca's focus shifted from the steely message in his eyes to the arrow's bright red feathers, the shaft's long straight line and finally the weapon's potentially lethal head. Then she thought of this man's lack of empathy—his obsession with self-enrichment. How could this superb body harbor such a depraved soul? How could Jack Reed live with himself?

Becca took the arrow from his hand, broke the shaft over a knee and, shaking inside, strode away.

Jack watched Becca Stevens's spectacular behind as she marched off in a fiery temper and had to smile.

When Becca had contacted his office hoping to meet, instinct had said to shake her off. If ever Jack set his sights on a target, he committed to that goal two hundred percent. No one and nothing would sway him. In certain circles, the term pathological was used to describe his drive.

No offense taken.

The same circles might suggest that his reasons for meeting Becca today had been selfish. That it was probable to very likely he would take advantage of his position in this Lassiter standoff for personal gain. And where Becca was concerned, Jack did mean personal.

As she disappeared over the rise, he smiled again.

What a woman.

His cell phone rang. Jack checked out the caller I.D. and, toeing Ms. Stevens's broken arrow aside, connected. "Logan. What've you got?"

"Just making sure we're still on track."

Coming from humble beginnings, Logan Whittaker had worked hard to build a successful career. As a partner at Drake, Alcott and Whittaker Attorneys based in downtown Cheyenne, Wyoming, Logan had looked after J. D. Lassiter's affairs, including the execution of J.D.'s last will and testament. The document had cast some challenges Logan's way. Some unanticipated rewards, as well. Through work associated with settling the will's terms, he had found his future wife.

"I've spoken with Angelica Lassiter again this morning," Jack said. "She's still going forward."

"You're sure about that? I've told Angelica more than once the will is airtight. J.D. was in his right mind when he drafted the terms. With majority voting interest, Evan McCain will remain chairman and CEO of Lassiter Media no matter how many punches she wants to throw. I thought she was finally coming around, listening to reason."

Jack headed back toward the shooting line. "Sure, she has reservations. Her father was a huge influence on her life. Even with him gone, it goes against the grain to disappoint him and battle that will. But her heart and soul are in that company, Logan. She has J.D.'s stubborn streak as well as his keen bent for business."

"How hard will you push her?"

"This isn't my first rodeo." When the attorney audibly exhaled, Jack wasn't fazed. "You're acting under strict instruction here."

"I'm aware of my obligations, damn it. This still leaves a god-awful taste in my mouth."

That all came with the territory…with being obligated, no matter what.

"No one said you had to like it," Jack said.

Logan huffed. "You're one hard-nosed son of a bitch, you know that?"

"That from a corporate lawyer." *Funny.*

As Jack reached back to draw an arrow from his quiver, Logan asked, "How did your meeting with Becca Stevens play out?"

Logan was aware of Becca's phone call and today's arrangements.

"She might run Lassiter Charity Foundation," Jack said, "but Becca is no Mother Teresa. She put on her boxing gloves and told me to back the hell away."

"Did you toss her off your property?"

Remembering the fire blazing in those beautiful green eyes, Jack held the phone between his ear and shoulder as he slotted the arrow's notch against his bow's string. "I would've asked her to stay for lunch if I thought she wouldn't try to run a butter knife through my heart."

"Will she be a problem?"

"Lord, I hope so."

Logan groaned. "For God's sakes, Jack. Tell me you plan to keep your pants on here."

"After the way you mixed Lassiter business up with pleasure, you're in no position to lecture."

When J.D. had bequeathed five million big ones to a mystery woman who didn't want to be found, Logan had not only tracked her down, damned if he hadn't taken her to bed, and more than once. Talk about calling the kettle black.

"I won't deny certain lines got blurred," Logan admitted. "But I fell in love with Hannah Armstrong and married her. I'll hand my resignation in to the bar the day anything approaching marriage enters your head."

Jack laughed. What an idea.

After the men disconnected, Jack resumed his stand behind the shooting line. He drew back the arrow and, enjoying the tension of the bowstring as he took aim, thought of Becca Stevens—the undisguised malice in her eyes, the sweeping conviction of her words. Then he imagined how darn good she would feel folded in his arms...how sweet her smooth, scented skin would taste beneath his lips. In his mind, Jack heard her whimper his name and then cry out as he sank into her again and again.

Jack released his shot and then shaded his brow to measure the result. When was the last time he'd missed a target's center gold ring? This arrow had sailed clean over the top.

Felicity Sinclair's blue eyes sparkled as she shifted her chair closer to the café table and lowered her voice. "Becca, I have something I need to ask."

"About Lassiter Media?"

As Lassiter Media's recently promoted vice president of public relations, Fee was always brimming with ideas. Since Becca's appointment with the Lassiter Charity Foundation two years ago, the women had worked closely. More than that—they'd become good friends, the kind who shared everything, during good times as well as bad.

Winding golden-blond hair behind a dainty ear, Fee explained, "My question has to do with Chance Lassiter."

"That would be your *fiancé* Chance Lassiter," Becca teased.

As Fee reached over to grip her friend's hand, the magnificent diamond on her third finger threw back light slanting in through the window.

"You were there when I needed to vent about that mess last month," she said. "I have to say, it feels a little strange calling Cheyenne home. I love L.A...."

"Well, you're here now. You'll simply have to visit often." Becca squeezed her hand. "Promise?"

"And you promise to drop in on us at the Big Blue."

"I'll bring my Stetson."

Chance Lassiter was J.D.'s nephew, the son of the billionaire's deceased younger brother, Charles. Chance had managed his uncle's world-famous cattle ranch—the Big Blue—and while he'd been rocked by J.D.'s unexpected death, he'd gladly accepted, via his uncle's will, controlling interest in the ranch he loved more than anything…although now, of course, his vivacious wife-to-be had taken pride of place in the charming cowboy's heart.

Fee sat back. "I can hardly wait for the wedding. Which brings me back to that question. Becca, would you be a bridesmaid?"

Emotion prickled behind Becca's eyes. Fee would make a *stunning* bride and, given her talent for organizing grand occasions, the ceremony was bound to be nothing short of amazing. Becca was even a little envious.

Marriage and starting a family were nowhere near a priority, but one day Becca hoped to find Mr. Right—a kindred spirit who got off on giving back and paying forward. This minute, however, all her energies were centered on helping the foundation survive the storm J.D.'s unexpected death and will had left behind.

Of course, there was *always* room for the wonderful women in her life and their very special requests.

Becca hugged her friend. "Fee, I would be honored to be a bridesmaid at your wedding."

The women discussed styles for dresses as well as flowers for bouquets before the conversation turned to a far less pleasant topic.

As coffees arrived, Fee asked, "Have you spoken with Jack Reed yet?"

Suddenly feeling queasy, Becca nodded. Fee knew that she had hoped to get in Jack's ear.

"The backyard of his Beverly Hills mansion houses an Olympic-standard archery field."

Fee's lip curled. "Your regular Robin Hood."

"The joke of the decade, right?" Becca pulled her decaf closer. "I let him know how his association with Angelica is weighing on Lassiter Media, not least of all the foundation. A lot of the funding comes from Lassiter accounts, but other benefactors are shutting doors in our face. While the notorious Jack Reed has a chance of pulling off a takeover bid and then tearing everything apart, we might as well have leprosy."

Fee flinched. "Jack does have a reputation."

Huge understatement. "He's the most ruthless corporate raider this country has given breath to. I hate to think of how quickly he'd chop up the company and sell off the pieces if he had a chance. He doesn't give a flying fig where or how the foundation ends up." Becca held her stomach when it churned again. "He's a scourge on mankind."

"You have to admit though…" Fee lifted her cup to her lips. "He is charismatic."

"If you can call a snake charismatic."

"And incredibly good-looking."

Becca huffed—and then gave it up. "Sure. The guy is hot, in a Jay Gatsby kind of way."

"Gatsby was gorgeous."

"Gatsby was a crook."

"Sweetie, let's face it. Jack Reed is *smoking*."

Becca's stomach pitched again. "I was taught that power should be used for good. If you have brains and position, for God's sake, help those less fortunate—even a *little* bit."

"Good luck convincing Jack Reed of that."

"Greed." Becca shuddered. "It's a disease." When the waitress delivered their coffees, she pointed to an item on the menu. "Can I have a caramel fudge brownie, please?"

As the waitress made a note and walked away, Fee studied her friend curiously. "Since when do you have a sweet tooth?"

"In school I was always the chubby kid who tried to get out of gym. If ever I felt anxious—upset—I'd reach for cake or candy."

Then she'd joined the Peace Corps and all that had changed. Her life had taken its sharpest turn yet.

Fee set her cup down. "Well, you're the poster girl for svelte now."

"That craving for sweet stuff doesn't win too often anymore. Don't worry," Becca said as the waitress delivered the brownie. "I'll fit into my bridesmaid's dress."

"I wouldn't care if you were a size two or a twenty." Fee had an awesome athletic build but she didn't judge any book by its cover. "I just hate to see you this rattled."

Becca bit into the brownie. As chocolate crumbs fell apart on her tongue, she almost sighed. She tried not to indulge; so many in this world did without. But, dear God, this was good.

"I believe in the foundation," she said, sucking caramel off a thumb. "I believe in the work it does. Do you know how much we've helped with homeless services, with youth camps, with disaster relief?"

When she slid over the plate to share, Fee broke off a corner of the brownie.

"Your team does an incredible job," Fee said and popped it in her mouth.

"And everyone on my staff wants to keep doing our job—raising funds, making a difference—one person and family at a time."

Fee's mouth twisted. "Unfortunately, it's not your company."

At the moment Lassiter Media was at the center of a tug-of-war primarily between Evan and Angelica, two people who ought to be working, and living, together, not pulling each other apart.

"J.D. couldn't have wanted this dissention within the family when he drew up his will."

"Given their connection," Fee added, "how hard she worked in the company the months before her father's death, I don't get how he left Angelica so little. It doesn't make sense."

Becca broke off more brownie and mulled as she chewed. "John Douglas Lassiter was a smart man," she reflected. "A good man with a big heart. The foundation was way more than a tax dodge to J.D. I *have* to believe he had a good reason for the way his will was arranged."

"He must have known Angelica would fight."

"Even her brothers are against her now." At first, Angelica's siblings had supported her attempts to find ways to challenge the will. No longer. "No one is left on her side."

"No one except Jack the Slasher Reed."

"For everyone's sakes, I hope she gives it up soon, before any more damage is done." To the family as well as the company, including the foundation.

"With Jack Reed egging her on, don't hold your breath."

An image formed in Becca's mind…Jack Reed with a quiver slung over his back. He looked so arrogant. So flat-out sexy and self-serving. Becca growled. "It all comes back to Jack."

"You're not finished with him, are you?"

"I can't give up." Becca pushed the plate aside. "I'm not made that way."

Fee sighed. "Problem is Jack Reed's not made that way, either."

Two

Jack waited until the end of the week and then buckled.

Dusting off a tux, he organized a ticket for the Lassiter Charity Foundation gala ball. By the time he'd finished at the office and then showered and drove over, he was unfashionably late. The keynote speaker had long since finished entertaining and educating the glittering crowd. Desserts had been served and suitable music wafted around the ballroom, coaxing couples onto a dance floor that sprawled beneath prisms of light cast by a spectacular Swarovski chandelier.

As he headed toward the VIP tables, Becca Stevens noticed him. Mild surprise registered on her face before she turned in her chair to gauge his approach. Loose, salon-tousled curls mantled her shoulders. Her ears and throat were free of jewels. Sitting proud and erect in a white strapless gown that accentuated her curves and teased the imagination, she gave an impression that lay somewhere between temptress and saint. When Jack stopped before her, she looked up at all six-plus feet of him and arched a brow.

"Did you notice?" she asked.

"That you look exquisite tonight?"

Her narrowing gaze sent a warning. *Don't flirt.*

"When you walked into the room," she explained, "people stopped talking. I think a lot stopped breathing. They don't expect to see you at a charity night. Although in this case they might—given it's a Lassiter Media event."

"Because I'm the big bad wolf here to gobble up everything I can sink my fangs into and then spit out the bones."

She shrugged a bare shoulder. "Not to put too fine of a point on it."

"Would it surprise you to know that I give to charity?"

"The Jack Reed Foundation for Chronic Self-Indulgence?"

He rubbed a corner of his grin. "You're cute, you know that?"

"Wait till I get started."

The only other couple left at the table was engrossed in a private conversation. If the room had indeed been distracted by his appearance, the socialites and Fortune 500 reps were back to mingling as far as Jack could tell.

He took the vacant seat next to Becca's. "When I donate, I do it anonymously."

Becca brought a glass of water to her lips. "How convenient."

"It's your job to blow this foundation's bugle. How much you give away, how much you help the disadvantaged. Publicity equals exposure, equals a greater chance of raising even more funds and getting the money to those who need it."

As the music swelled and lights dimmed more, he leaned closer and caught the scent of her perfume—a hint of red apple, feminine. Way too sexy for her own good—at least where he was concerned.

"But tell me," he went on, "if you had as much personal wealth as I do, would you need to go around bleating to everyone how generous you were?"

"I will never have that much personal wealth. Don't want it. Don't need it. I'm nothing like you. Not in any way, shape or form." When his gaze dropped to skim her lips, she frowned slightly before pushing to her feet. "Don't even think about going there."

No denying he was attracted to Becca Stevens. He had wanted to tip closer, sample those lips, invite her to help fuel the spark. If he wasn't mistaken—and Jack was rarely wrong—there was a part of Becca that wanted that, too.

"Am I that obvious?" he asked, getting to his feet.

"You're ridiculously easy to read."

"In certain things."

"I'll give you a list. Tell me what I'm missing."

As waiters served coffee, Jack crossed his arms. "Go ahead."

"You have an insatiable thirst for money. Correction. For *power*. You like expensive toys. Jets and yachts and prestige cars. You enjoy beautiful women hanging off your arm, the more the merrier. Above all else, you love calling the shots. Being the king of your cancerous castle."

Jack frowned.

Ouch.

"I like being the boss," he said. "So do all CEOs. So did J.D."

"You're missing my point. And, sorry, but you're not in J.D.'s league."

"He might argue with you on that."

Her look was almost pitying. "Modesty is so not your strong suit."

"Perhaps you'd care to find out what is."

"You know, for a smart guy, you just don't get it."

When she breezed out of the room, Jack followed her onto the terrace. He found her standing by a railing, facing a twinkling downtown view. A breeze caught a layer of her gown's skirt; gossamer-thin fabric billowed out, ruffling behind her like filmy wings.

As he headed over, she tossed him an annoyed glance before gripping the railing like she wanted to wring someone's neck. "You can't take a hint, can you?"

"Let's not play that kind of game," he drawled. "You wanted me to follow. You're just not sure how to handle things now that I have."

She faced him. "I'm passionate about my work at the foundation. More passionate than I've felt about anything before in my life, and that's saying something."

"It's how a person uses her passion that counts."

"How about for good rather than evil?"

Most people thought of Jack Reed that way. Evil incarnate. Difference was that Becca wasn't afraid to tell him point-blank.

Hell, she was right. Everyone was. If he could get his paws on Lassiter Media, if he could truly sink his teeth into a vein, he wouldn't let go until he'd drained it all. That was his profession. What he did best.

But with Becca Stevens looking at him as if malevolence might be contagious, for just a second Jack almost hoped he wouldn't get the chance. A part of him actually wanted to let this colossal Lassiter Media opportunity slide off into the water.

Of course, that wasn't possible. Wasn't—*sane*. Neither was continuing to annoy poor Ms. Stevens. It wasn't her fault she was caught up in this fight, any more than Jack could help the part he had to play.

"It's time my black cape and I flapped away before the

first hint of dawn turns us into dust." He affected a bow. "Good night, Becca."

She caught up with him at the entrance back into the ballroom, slotting herself between his chest and the door. Jack didn't know whether to smile and relax or frisk her for a wooden stake.

"What if I show you how serious I am?" she said. "I'll prove to you how much good this foundation does. Have you ever visited homeless shelters, soup kitchens? If you see firsthand, you'd have to understand. You can't be *that* big of a monster...can you?"

"You mean it's possible I might have human emotions after all?"

When she allowed a small smile, Jack grinned, too. "Give me a month," she said, "and I'll change your mind."

"Change my mind about what?"

"About dismantling Lassiter Media's assets."

Interesting. "You think Angelica and I can win?"

Becca lifted her chin. "Four weeks."

"One day."

"One week."

"On one condition."

"Name it."

What the hell. "I'd rather show you."

He slid a hand around her waist and drew her in as his mouth dropped over hers.

She went stiff against him. Hands balled into fists against his chest. He waited for her to tear away and call him every name under the sun. Short of her scratching his eyes out, Jack figured it was worth it.

Instead, her fists melted and palms slowly spread before her fingers knotted, winding into his jacket lapels. Then, making a strangled sound in her throat, she pressed in plumb against him. Jack relaxed into it, too.

As his palm on her back tugged her closer, his other

hand slipped beneath the curls at the warm base of her neck. Gradually her lips parted under his. Kneading her nape, he tilted his head at more of an angle at the same time the tip of his tongue slid by her teeth.

She stiffened again and this time broke away. Short of breath, eyes wild, she wiped her mouth on her arm. Then she called him a name Jack had been called more than once but never by a lady.

"What was *that* supposed to be?"

Jack ran a hand back through his hair. "You tell me."

She siphoned down air, half composed herself. "Fine," she said. "I will. That was a mistake. A big fat *never again*."

"Unless you decide you want to."

She stabbed a finger at his nose. "You repulse me."

"Do you want to hear my condition or not?"

Puzzled, she blinked twice. "Condition?"

"To give you one week to change my mind."

Her throat bobbed as she swallowed and pushed curls back from her brow. "Oh. Right."

"My condition is that we are civil toward each other."

She muttered, "Figures that would be your idea of civil."

It wasn't the time to mention that she had kissed him right back.

"Do we have an agreement?" Jack hesitated and then ribbed her anyway. "Or are you afraid you might find my dark charm irresistible?"

Her slim nostrils flared. "I'd sooner sell my soul to the devil."

"Be careful what you wish for." Jack pulled open the door and noise from the ballroom seeped out. "I'll collect you from your office Monday, ten a.m. sharp."

"I'll arrange my own transport. I'll meet you—"

"Uh-uh. I make the rules. The challenge for you now is to change the game."

"Using any means available?"

Jack smiled into her spirited green gaze. "What an appealing thought."

Three

Early Monday, as Jack finished up his first call of the working week, the vice president of Reed Incorporated crossed over to his desk. A financial dynamo with a killer background in trading, Sylvia Morse set her hands on her hips.

"What exactly are you doing?"

Sylvia had been standing inside his office door for the past few minutes, so, trick question?

"What do you mean what am I doing?" Jack asked.

"I want the lowdown. No B.S. Not to me. You just got off the phone from Angelica Lassiter—*again*. You've moved mountains to acquire every Lassiter Media share you can lay your hands on. You'd do anything to get a hold of hers."

Sylvia's brunette razor-cut looked somehow spikier today, and her normally light gray gaze was definitely darker. He almost asked whether her caffeine addiction had escalated to substances that caused memory loss or confusion, but then Jack remembered her brother was in rehab again and went with the direct approach instead.

He set down his pen. "What the hell is up with you this morning?"

"You're in bed with Angelica Lassiter," Sylvia went on, "to help her regain control of J.D.'s company."

"Metaphorically speaking, absolutely."

"And?"

"Sylvia, you've been my right hand here for five years. Nothing's changed."

"So, you intend to buy up, buy in and then put into play the most efficient, financially rewarding way to sell off the various pieces of Lassiter Media. Except that isn't Angelica Lassiter's plan."

Jack slumped. *Et tu, Sylvia?* "I thought our moral compasses were in sync."

"This is different."

"It's never different." He picked up the pen, put his head down. "Trust me."

"God knows I want to, but something's missing. Unless you're more ruthless than even I thought, and I know you pretty well."

"Better than anyone."

"I'm on your side, Jackie-boy. Always. But, while you'd never admit it publicly, even you must have limits. J. D. Lassiter was a friend. You'd call in on each other's homes in Cheyenne. I thought that kind of relationship would put a spin on things."

"You thought wrong."

"So, feelings never get in the way of business."

Jack got to his feet. "Feelings don't get in the way of anything. Period."

He moved to a nearby credenza. Last week, he'd been sorting through a spread of figures on a boat company he was keen to acquire. Easy money—or it would be in a few months after he'd taken over and maximized the various resources.

"I value your work," Jack told Sylvia, thumbing through the top pages of Baldwin Boats' annual financials. "I value *you*. But if ever you decide you want to, you know—move on—I'd only ever wish you well."

"Where in blazes would you ever find another me?"

Jack returned her mocking grin. "Wouldn't be easy." Then it clicked. "Oh, okay. Sure. I get what this is about."

Her face opened up. "You do?"

"You've been working day and night on the Lassiter deal. Crazy hours. Follows you want a bigger cut when the demolition ball starts swinging."

The intensity in her gaze deepened again before her expression eased and a crooked smile appeared. "Guess you are as big a hard-ass as they say." She crossed over, scanned a spreadsheet. "Baldwin Boats."

Pushing the prickly issue of Lassiter Media aside, Jack nodded. "I'm ready to move on it."

"I spoke with David Baldwin late Friday. He wants you to meet with him. He asked if you'd like a tour of the factory."

Jack had already seen the factory. Damn it, he knew all he needed to know.

He hung his head and winced. "I hate this part."

"You mean the part where a struggling businessman who's put his entire life into a company thinks there might be a chance of talking you into injecting some much-needed capital and becoming partners?"

"Yeah, Sylvia. That part. I've told him we'll put together a good offer. The best he'll get before his company is forced into bankruptcy. I'm not interested in having a beer with the boys out back."

David Baldwin had recently made an appointment to discuss his situation. His company, while not huge, had ongoing contracts and sizeable assets. Baldwin Boats was also in financial strife with no easy way out. Same story. Bad economy, rising costs and taxes. Jack had said he thought they could do business. *His* kind of business, not Baldwin's. On that, he'd been clear.

Baldwin made beautiful boats but Jack wasn't in the manufacturing trade. To his way of thinking, Baldwin could either come out of this with something via Reed Incorporated's offer, or he could walk away with nothing due to bankruptcy. Despite popular opinion, Jack wasn't completely heartless, even where Lassiter Media was concerned. He hoped David Baldwin grabbed the buoy he had tossed rather than clinging to blind hope and going under.

"Just let him know," Jack said, "that we'll have a firm offer to him by end of the month."

When Sylvia turned to leave, he called after her.

"Just a heads-up. Becca Stevens paid me a visit."

"The director of Lassiter Media's Charity Foundation, right?"

"She threw out a challenge. If I gave her some time, she would change my mind about going after the company."

"You're joking."

"She wants to show me where the money goes."

"And you said go jump."

"I gave her a week."

Sylvia's jaw dropped. It took her time to recover. "You schedule your days down to the minute."

"If I play my cards right, I might be able to glean some valuable inside information."

Sylvia was shaking her head. "I've run checks on everyone of any note at the company. Becca Stevens is former foster care and post-grad Peace Corps. She might look delectable on the outside but that woman is no cream puff. If you're planning to ensnare Becca with your charms, tread carefully. She's smart and she's tough and she'll do anything to win."

Jack ran a finger and thumb down his tie. "We should get on like two peas in a pod." Catching the time on his watch, he moved to grab his jacket. "I'm meeting with Joe Rivers to discuss the logistics on that opportunity in China, and then I'm off to meet Ms. Stevens."

"Off to *seduce* Ms. Stevens, you mean." Sylvia angled her head. "Unless she's a step ahead of you."

"How so?" He shrugged into his jacket.

"Maybe she plans to do the seducing."

"To work her way into my heart and save her foundation?"

"I'm not kidding. My information says she's extremely resourceful."

He winked and swung open the door for them both. "Lord, I hope so."

As Jack Reed's luxury black sedan swerved off Sunset and into the Lassiter Media Building's forecourt, Becca strode over and swung open the passenger-side door. She settled into the soft leather seat while, hands locked on the wheel, Jack assessed her quizzically.

At the gala ball, he'd caught her off guard. In a designer tuxedo he'd been born to wear, every aspect of his star quality had been amplified tenfold. The white slash of his smile had almost knocked Becca off her chair. By the time he'd stopped at the table, her heart was thudding in her throat, in her ears. She thought she'd hid his effect on her pretty well.

Until that kiss.

Their head-spinning, utterly unforgivable kiss.

Today Becca was prepared. Alert and armed and ready for anything.

"Nice ride," she said, buckling up. "Smells new." And

while she would never admit it out loud, Jack smelled good, too. Fresh and woodsy and one hundred percent male.

"I know when we agreed to do this I said *my rules,* but I didn't expect you to wait outside for me. I'd have come up to collect you."

"Time is money."

"Well, that's…considerate of you."

"I was talking about the foundation's time and money."

The uncertain look on his face cleared and his dark eyes gleamed as he grinned. "Of course you were."

When he flicked a questioning glance at her legs, Becca secretly quivered. The look wasn't meant to be intimate, but her body didn't seem to know the difference. Warmth washed through her veins, the same shot of heat that had made rubber bands of her ligaments when Jack had kissed her that night.

Becca's hands bunched in her lap.

Don't think about that now.

"Do you wear jeans to the office often?" he asked, steering onto the road.

"Depends what I have planned for the day."

She sounded cool and collected despite her nails digging into her palms. His nearest arm and thigh were too close. Even in the air-conditioning, his body heat was tangible, enough to make her upper lip and hairline sweat.

"Where are we headed?" he asked, changing up gears.

"A high school." Nodding at the stoplights, Becca set her mind to the task. "Next right here."

"A school, huh? Someone need a new gym?"

She studied his profile, the hawkish nose, that confident air. "You really have no idea, do you?"

"I thought that's what this week was about. Giving me a clue."

She planned to do a truckload more than that.

"How well do you remember your teenage years?"

she asked. "You'd have done well in sport. Football's my guess." He only smiled. "You got good grades, too, right? I bet you didn't have to try."

"Chemistry was tricky."

"But you knew what you liked. What resonated. And your parents could afford an Ivy League school."

"I worked hard when I got there."

"What kind of car did you drive?"

He named a luxury German make.

"Fresh off the assembly line?" she asked.

His laugh was warm and deep. "You think you can guilt me out, Becca?"

"I hope I can open your eyes."

He looked across at her again and this time when he took in her jeans, Becca sensed he was labeling her, slotting her into another compartment in his head. The very idea set her teeth on edge.

"You didn't come from money," he said.

He didn't need to know the whole story—or not at this early stage in the game.

"My parents own a bakery."

He threw her a surprised look and held it before concentrating again on the traffic.

"I'm one of four," she went on. "We kids were taught that we needed to take responsibility for others in society who were less fortunate. Giving back and being community-minded are the secret not only to a happy life but also a happier world. During my senior year, I volunteered at hospitals and nursing homes…."

Attention on the road, his gaze had gone glassy. Becca cleared her throat.

"Am I boring you, Jack?"

"You could never bore me." He rubbed his freshly shaven jaw, which still had the shadow of persistent stubble. "It's just that I've traveled a few miles since school."

She appealed to Jack Reed's ego. "I can't imagine how much you've learned since then. How much you could pass on."

"Is that what we're doing? You want me to give a talk to schoolkids about aiming for the stars?"

"A fair percentage of the kids we'll see today have battled depression and suicidal thoughts and some have even attempted to end their own lives."

From the way a pulse had suddenly begun to pop in his cheek, finally she had his attention.

She indicated a driveway. "In there."

The public secondary high school had around three thousand students, grades nine through twelve. Its multistory red-brick buildings, landscaped with soaring palm trees, had been used as filming locations for several movies and TV shows. After parking the car, they headed for an area by the front chain-link fence where a mass of students had gathered. The kids were cheering as a stream of riders on bicycles flew past in a blur of Lycra color and spinning wheels. A couple of students waved a big sign: *Ride for U.S.*

"Do you ride a bike, Jack?" Becca asked over the hoots and applause from the excited mob jostling around them.

"Not one with pedals. Not for a while."

"These people are riding from coast to coast to bring awareness and help to teenagers who can't see a light at the end of their tunnel. Whose parents might be alcoholics, prostitutes, drug addicts or dealers. A lot of those kids bring themselves up. They might be taught to fetch drugs or another bottle of booze from the cabinet."

As the last of the bikes shot past, Jack gazed on, looking strangely indifferent. Detached.

She tried again. "The Lassiter Foundation donates to this cause every year, and we help decide where and how funds raised ought to be spent."

He took out a pair of shades from his inside breast pocket and perched them on his nose. "A big job."

"Not compared to the effort this bunch puts in."

Some students were fooling around with a football. When a toss went off track, Jack reached and effortlessly caught the ball before hurling it back to the boys. Then, impassive again, he straightened his shades.

"You don't have any children?" she asked.

"I'm not married."

"The two don't necessarily go hand in hand."

"No children."

"That you know of."

He exhaled. "Right."

The crowd started to head back into the building. "How freaky would it be to find out that you'd fathered a child say twenty years ago when you were cruising around in that gleaming new Beamer, acing your assignments, planning out your future with waves of twenty-four-carat-gold glitter."

"I might have a reputation, but I've always been responsible where sex is concerned."

"Right there we have a difference in understanding. How can a big-time player be responsible where sex in concerned?"

His smile was thin. "Takes practice."

"We're getting off topic. Point is that from day one you led a privileged life. Most kids aren't that lucky. Most children could use a hand on their way to reaching adulthood."

Inside the gymnasium, she and Jack sat to one side at the back in the bleachers while the leader of Ride for U.S. addressed the students. Tom Layton was a professional counselor Becca knew through various channels. He had incredible insight into the minds of young adults, a gift he used to full advantage. As he spoke to the audience,

Tom and Becca made eye contact. Tom winked to say hi but didn't miss a beat.

"Good, isn't he?" she whispered across to Jack. "Everything seems so *life or death* to teens. Tom gets that. A child needs all his strength going forward because the real test is later in life when he has to follow his own star, when he needs to develop a thick skin toward those who might want to trash his dream, for whatever reason."

Minus the sunglasses now, Jack trained his hooded gaze on her. "Would it surprise you to learn that you and I aren't so different, Becca?"

"It would surprise the living hell out of me."

His eyebrows drew together and damned if she didn't sense something real shift in Jack Reed. Not compassion or empathy exactly. That would have been too much to ask. It was more of a fleeting *connection* that fell through her fingertips, like loose grains of sand, before she could truly grasp it.

While Tom listed signs that everyone should watch for when identifying a peer who needed help, Becca scanned the audience. The geeks up front were all ears, some even taking notes. The lot in the middle alternated between sneaking looks at smartphones and zoning out, daydreaming about extracurricular activities. The mob in the back— the ones who really needed to listen—were restless. It was difficult to see a bright future when home life sucked everything into a vortex of gray. She and Tom wanted to help change that.

Thirty minutes later, as the principal thanked his guests and a round of applause went up, Jack immediately stood to stretch his spine. Becca looked up the entire length of him. God, he was tall.

"Still awake?" she asked, standing, too.

"Sure." He stretched again. "Coffee would be good though."

As they headed down the bleacher aisle, she helped bring the bigger picture into focus.

"The foundation works with school counselors across the country to get help to students who are under imminent threat. Who need our help now. This minute. We put on camps where they can talk about their problems in a safe and encouraging environment. Where they can share everything with others they identify with. It's important these kids know they're not alone."

At the bottom on the bleachers, Jack held up a hand. "Excuse me a moment? I need to make a call."

Okay. She'd drowned him with information, trying to make every second count. Now she needed to ease her foot off the pedal. Mix it up a bit.

"No problem," she said. "Go ahead. I'll wait here."

Jack drew out his cell and thumbed in a number as he strolled across the floor. By the time he'd disconnected, he'd wound back and was approaching a group who included Tom Layton. When the two men shook hands and spoke, Becca debated whether or not to join them. But they only talked for a moment before Tom sent a friendly wave her way and let Jack go. As Jack drew closer, she couldn't hide her smile.

"That was nice," she said.

"Sure. Nice guy." Jack rested his hand on her arm and eyed the exit. "Let's go."

Logic told Becca to remove herself from his touch. This wasn't a date.

Then again, giving her a guiding hand wasn't exactly an inappropriate gesture, either. If she wanted the chance to push her case going forward, she had to choose her battles. Jack had accepted her challenge, but he could walk away at any time.

And, secretly...

A part of her liked the contact. Crazy, dangerous, stupid. Still, there it was.

As he led her toward the gym doors, Becca made a suggestion.

"We could go back to the office for that coffee. My barista skills are renowned in that building."

"You're not afraid of being hit by a grenade," he said, "or ambushed by gunfire? That's why you waited outside this morning, isn't it? You wanted to keep this arrangement and the questions as quiet as possible."

Her step almost faltered. "I told you why I met you downstairs."

"You're not worried some people might think you're getting too friendly with the foe?"

"If I was worried about my reputation, I wouldn't invite you back, now, would I?" Sliding her arm away from his, she turned his assumption on its head. "Maybe it's you who's afraid to front up at Lassiter Media."

His slanted grin oozed sex appeal. "Yeah," he said. "That must be it."

As they entered the parking lot, Becca took stock. She'd decided to ease back on the info dump, and she'd got rattled at the idea of her loyalties ever being questioned, but she still needed to keep the dialogue open and evolving. She had to keep Jack close. *So, big breath and moving on.*

"Now that's settled," she said, walking alongside of him, "are we on for coffee?"

"If Danishes are involved."

"You're a fan?"

"Can you spell cheese, blueberry, apple toffee?"

Suddenly Becca could taste all her favorites. "How about cinnamon or custard?"

"Now you're talking."

"With my family owning a bakery, there was lots of cake growing up. *Too* much."

He gave her an odd look and then smiled. "You can never have too much cake."

Becca could have argued. She also wanted to know what that strange look was about. Instead she smiled as he opened the car door for her. If she let him in a little more, maybe he would open up to her, too. And then surely light and a sprinkling of goodness would fall among the shadows. Even where blackhearted Jack Reed was concerned.

Jack parked in a space outside of the Lassiter Media Building. After switching off the ignition, he lifted his chin to loosen his tie. He was serious about needing a coffee—extra strong. At each turn this morning, he'd been taken off guard.

Firstly, he was sure Sylvia had said that Becca had been a foster kid. Was she lying about the bakery? Something hinky was going on there.

Second, he, too, was a benefactor of Ride for U.S. When Tom Layton had spotted him and Becca in the bleachers together, Jack had seen speculation flare in the younger man's eyes. It wasn't a reach to think Tom had wondered whether he and Becca had partnered up in some charity-minded capacity. So, before Tom had the chance to wander over and all kinds of questions were asked, Jack had made an excuse and had "bumped" into him. Then, on the quiet, he'd let Tom know nothing had changed. *No one* needed to know who Reed Incorporated gave to, when, how or particularly why—unless it was the taxman.

If Becca wanted to stand behind general consensus and believe his character was a step away from sludge, Jack was used to being pegged as a villain. Hell, wearing that label where Becca was concerned was probably best. When the Lassiter deal went his way and the ax began to fall all around her, she might be hurt but at least she wouldn't be surprised.

On the upside, he had heard everything she'd said about problems facing young adults. Depression, self-harm, suicide...he wished he could wave a wand and all the damage—past, present and future—would be fixed.

Becca got out of the car before Jack had a chance to swing around and open her door.

"Will we personally choose our Danishes?" she asked over the roof of the car. "Or should we have them delivered?"

On the way back from the school, she'd mentioned a good bakery near the office.

"We'll go have a look," he said.

"Cheese, blueberry and apple toffee, right?"

Slipping on sunglasses, he met her at the trunk. "And cinnamon and custard."

She laughed, an effervescent, sexy sound that suited her far better than a scowl. "Just how much can you eat? Or am I buying for the whole office?"

"I'm buying," he said. "Might as well throw in a couple of chocolate chip muffins while we're at it."

"Now that's getting dangerous." They headed off toward the mall via the building's entrance. "And it's *my* treat. No argument. You're my guest." She playfully eyed him up and down. "A guest with a very big appetite."

"And growing by the minute."

Her smile changed in a knowing, measured way at the same time her gaze flicked to his mouth. Every one of Jack's extremities began to tingle.

Maybe she's the one doing the seducing.

Earlier, he had scoffed at Sylvia's suggestion, but the idea of Becca Stevens as calculating seductress out to save the world wasn't so far-fetched. Would she think that flirting, or even sleeping with him, might gain her information...curry favor...change his mind? After the kiss they had shared, he knew her hormones wouldn't object even if her conscience did.

Out of the corner of his eye, Jack saw a woman emerge from the building's main entrance. The slender build, dark brown hair and matching eyes were unmistakable. Angelica Lassiter was so absorbed in her thoughts, she almost ran into them without noticing. Recognizing Jack first, she sagged and let out a ragged sigh.

"Thank God. How did you know I'd be here?" she asked. Then she saw Becca.

Angelica was strong-willed, like her dad. But right now, with those dark-brown eyes wide and questioning, she looked as if she was teetering on an edge.

Jack spoke to Becca first. "Can we do this later?"

She said, "Of course," before offering Angelica an awkward goodbye. As Becca moved inside the building, Jack looped his arm through Angelica's.

"C'mon. Let's walk."

Four

"What are you doing with Becca Stevens?" Angelica asked as Jack ushered her away from the Lassiter Media Building and down the busy boulevard sidewalk.

"Becca's worried about the foundation's future," he said.

Angelica nodded deeply. "She does a brilliant job there. Her heart is totally in the right place. But, Jack, don't think for a minute she's on our side. She doesn't like you. Given our association, I'm sure she doesn't like me much at the moment, either."

Angelica could easily have grown up a spoiled pain. She'd come along later in Ellie Lassiter's life, after J.D. and his wife had been warned against ever trying to conceive. Ellie had died just days after giving birth to a healthy baby girl. Elevated blood pressure had brought on a stroke.

Years earlier, Ellie and J.D. had adopted her orphaned nephews, Sage and Dylan. After Ellie's death, J.D. and the boys had showered all their love and attention on Angelica, who had developed into a remarkably caring, career-minded woman.

It was no secret that J.D. had been grooming his daughter to take over Lassiter Media. When J.D. had died suddenly from a massive coronary, everyone was shocked to hear his final wishes at the will's reading. But, one by one, all had accepted the inexplicable terms. All except Angelica and, of course, Jack.

"Yep, Becca supports Evan."

"And if you want her to switch camps," Angelica went on, "you're wasting your time. When that woman makes up her mind about something, there's no changing it. And frankly, Jack, I don't see any point in trying."

"You've got it mixed up. Becca came to me. She wants me to see where the foundation's money goes. All the good it does."

He thought better of admitting he was hoping to pick up some Lassiter intel along the way. He wouldn't add to the tally of his baser tactics where Angelica's opinion of him was concerned.

She was mulling over his words. "Becca wants to inspire you enough that you'll back off from any takeover bid, and all the bad publicity and doubt plaguing the foundation will disappear along with you."

She stopped and sat heavily down on a vacant bench at a bus stop.

"I *hate* that the company is suffering," she said. "I hate that my family can barely look at me anymore." She exhaled a shaky breath as he sat alongside of her. "It's getting to me, Jack. Grinding me down until my head feels like it might explode."

"Trust me," he said. "We're in a good place with this."

"I rang Dylan this morning, a sisterly call to see how he and Jenna are doing."

Dylan had got involved with Jenna Montgomery, a florist in Cheyenne. Jack had heard that the couple had weathered some severe relationship storms before recently tying the knot.

"Of course, the conversation swung onto the will," Angelica went on. "I got so stirred up, I could have hit something. Out of everyone, I never thought Dylan would turn against me. We were so close when we were young. I thought we still were."

After high school, Dylan had set sail to see the world. Odd jobs in restaurants had grown into head chef opportunities in premiere establishments. Five years ago, J.D. asked him to head the Lassiter Grill Group with restaurants in L.A., Vegas, Chicago and now their hometown, Cheyenne. He'd inherited complete control of the restaurant business when J.D. died.

"Dylan told me again," Angelica said, "that I needed to accept Dad's wishes. That I should bury the hatchet and get on with my life." Staring into the noisy downtown traffic, she bit her lip and shook her head. "I needed to talk to Evan. Thrash it out. Know what he said? Evan said I should settle down. Sitting in *my* chair, in *my* office. Can you believe it?"

As a tear rolled down her cheek, Jack fished out a pressed handkerchief from his inside breast pocket.

Gritting her teeth, Angelica dabbed her face. "I can't get my mind around the fact that Evan somehow conspired with my father to do this. Or maybe Evan somehow conspired against us both."

Jack wanted to put his arm around her. Squeeze her hand. But Angelica didn't need sympathy. She needed firm direction. He sat forward, elbows on thighs, fingers thatched between knees.

"Evan's right," he said.

As the 302 bus growled by, she shot Jack a glance. "Excuse me?"

"You do need to settle down. Then you need to refocus and never let that target out of your sights. You can't afford to let emotion get in the way."

"Just sometimes, Jack…sometimes I wonder whether we're doing the right thing. Whether it's worth it."

"You wonder whether you ought to give up your inheritance because Sage and Dylan don't approve?" Pulling out all the stops, Jack turned toward her. "Sage was never close to J.D. He's a billionaire in his own right, for God's sakes, and yet he got twenty-five percent of Lassiter Media in the will. And Dylan? Why, he's happy as a pig in mud since he's snagged controlling interest of the Lassiter Grill Group. Then there's you. J.D.'s only child through blood. His little princess. Tell me how the hell it works when you get a lousy ten percent and the man you trusted enough to want to marry walks away with controlling voting interest of *your* father's company." Jack sneered. "I don't give a rat's furry behind whether or not Sage or Dylan or anyone else approves of your attempt to get what's rightfully yours."

Angelica's shoulders squared slightly and she blinked several times as if her eyes might be stinging.

"I miss Dad so much," she said. "I wish I could talk to him now. Let him make sense of it all. I'm torn between wanting to fold and being outraged that he could embarrass and hurt me like this. I worked my rear end off for that company. It was all I thought, ate. *Slept.*" She swallowed back emotion and brushed away another tear. "I'm just so tired of it all."

Jack almost groaned aloud. He'd valued J.D.'s friendship, but if he'd been alive and standing in front of him now, Jack would have plowed him in the jaw, what Jack stood to make out of this deal be damned.

Angelica dabbed her cheek again. "I'm a wimp."

"Hey, would I team up with a wimp?"

When he bumped her shoulder, she almost grinned.

"Sylvia and I are working nonstop," he said, "finding ways to boost our position in the company's shares. It won't be long now. We're almost there. Okay?"

A genuine smile flickered at the corners of her mouth before her gaze narrowed, searching his.

"In the past, you've only ever wanted to tear down and sell off companies you'd acquired. Why is Lassiter Media any different?"

"You really need to ask?"

"Everyone's asking."

"J.D. was a close friend. I've known you since you were a skinny kid with braids. I'm doing precisely, to a *T*, what your father would want me to do."

"Except it goes against his final wishes."

"That can't have been his intent. Search your heart and tell me you don't agree."

Her gaze narrowed again.

"You would never betray me, would you, Jack?"

As a shiver ran up his spine, Jack looked her dead in the eye. "No, Angelica," he said. "I would never betray you."

Jack followed Angelica back to the Lassiter family mansion, which sat on two acres of Beverly Hills north of Sunset. J.D. had bought the Spanish Colonial revival twenty years ago when he'd created the L.A. office. Built in the 1930s, the mansion retained its original wrought-iron detail, leaded glass and homemade Spanish tiles. In recent years, however, Angelica had contributed much in the way of decorating its 11,000 feet of luxury living space. It had been more her home than J.D.'s.

When Jack and Angelica began to go over some figures and she asked him to stay for lunch, of course, he accepted. He even helped her prepare enough egg salad sandwiches to feed ten. Then they sat and ate in the lanai, taking in the sparkling pool and the flawless blue sky of late summer. By the time they had talked through everything and Angelica felt positive again about going forward, the sun was arcing toward the west.

As she accompanied Jack through the living room with its soaring ceiling to the front entrance, for the hundredth time he considered the part he was playing in this unfolding drama. Complex and uncomfortable, even for him. Still, as he had said to Angelica earlier, they need only keep their eyes on the target.

"I shouldn't have kept you this long." Angelica looked weary, resting her cheek against the opened door edge as Jack stepped onto the extravagant porch.

"I'm here anytime you need me."

"Becca Stevens must be wondering where you got to."

"She probably welcomed the break."

"I doubt that."

When Angelica sent him a fond smile, Jack held her shoulder. "You'll be okay."

"You were always a good friend to my father...to me. I don't know what I'd do without you."

"You'll never have to worry about that."

There was a spring in Jack's step as he crossed to his car. He had helped Angelica—or *not* helped, depending on which team a person rooted for. On top of that, even after having his fill of egg salad, Jack was still fanging for those Danishes.

Steering out onto the main road, he put through a call to the Lassiter Foundation and gave his name. He was transferred to Becca's assistant.

"Sorry, Mr. Reed. Ms. Stevens left for the day."

Jack checked the dash clock. A little after four. "She's gone home?" he asked.

"I couldn't say."

He reverse head-butted the seat. *Damn.*

"Do you have her private number?"

"Sorry, sir. I can't give that out."

Jack knew he could get it easily enough. Not the point. Nothing was more important to Becca than saving her foundation, which translated into putting all her efforts into trying to talk him around. Surely her nose wasn't put out because Angelica had needed him earlier.

So, what had come up that was so urgent? Was Becca playing hard to get? He wasn't that desperate for Danish.

When his cell rang a minute later, he connected without checking the ID.

It wasn't Becca.

"Hey, Jack. David Baldwin here."

Jack flinched but put a smile in his voice. "Hey. How's it going, David?"

"Call me Dave. Have you got a few minutes? I'd like to show you something."

"Sylvia already mentioned another factory tour."

"She let me know. You've seen enough there."

"And you'll have an offer by end of the month." Silence echoed down the line. "Dave, you there?"

"I wanted to speak with you about a personal matter."

Damn it. He should've checked that caller ID. "I'm not sure I can help with any personal issues."

"Actually it's about me helping you."

"I'm tied up at the moment, but sit tight and we'll get that offer—"

"This is about family, Jack. It's about…a journey."

Jack had heard it all before in a hundred different ways from just as many different people. The times they had spoken, David Baldwin had come across as a good guy who'd worked hard and considered his employees to be just that…family. Now, he wanted Jack to get involved, drag his financial butt out of the fire and save his business. Save the day.

And, hey, there was something about David Baldwin that gave Jack pause. Something in the deep brown of his eyes that made him care. But this association could end only one way and that was not with the two of them sharing Christmas dinners.

"I'll be in touch soon," Jack said. "Another call's coming through. Take care."

He disconnected. A single beat later, pain ripped through his chest—a stab followed by one almighty twist. Stopping at lights, he winced, massaging the spot.

Not heartburn or, God forbid, a heart attack. Just this Lassiter issue getting to him. The Baldwin business, too. If David wanted to save his family, best of luck. Jack couldn't help.

And, while she might never accept it—while she would want to see his head on a spike when this was done—Jack couldn't help Becca Stevens, either.

The next morning, Jack's cell phone woke him.

Rubbing his eyes, Jack grabbed it, checked the caller ID—lesson learned—and connected.

"Jack?" Becca sounded puzzled. "Did I wake you?"

He sat up, ran a hand through his hair. The bedside clock read eight-oh-five. *Holy crap.* He always had trouble getting to sleep, but what the hell time had he finally nodded off last night?

"I thought I'd call early," she went on. "I have a plan."

Jack smothered a yawn. "I like plans."

"Can I come over and tell you about it?"

"I thought you might have been, well…"

"Pissed at you after ditching me yesterday? I understand your situation with Angelica. She feels backed into a corner."

"The only way out is to fight."

"Or to accept. Even forgive."

He swung his feet over and onto the floor. "Ultimately, that's up to her."

"It'd help if you stopped pushing her."

Jack grinned. "I thought you said you understood."

He heard her sigh. At least she didn't argue.

"What time can I come over?" she asked.

She certainly was eager. "Why not the office?"

"It'd save time."

He couldn't argue with that. "I'll just jump in the shower."

It was on the tip of his tongue to suggest that he'd wait for her. *Bad Jack.*

"See you in thirty then," she said.

Naked, he crossed to the bathroom. "I'll be here." *With bells on.*

Jack answered his booming doorbell wearing tatty jeans that hung low on his hips. He hadn't bothered to put on a shirt. When he lifted an arm to lean against the jamb and his epic six-pack firmed up even more, Becca could have drooled.

Look into his eyes. Not the big, bronzed chest or that strip of skin south of his navel, damn it. Look at his eyes.

"Morning," he said. "You're late."

A lousy ten minutes. And she wouldn't give him the satisfaction of asking where the rest of his clothes were, either. Even his feet were bare; who knew toes could be sexy?

The other time she had visited, an older man with an impeccable air had seen her through to the back lawn. "I thought the butler would answer the door," she said.

"Merv's not a butler." His arm slid down as he stepped back to allow her inside. "He looks after things for me on the home front. It's his day off."

"Did you grow up having a person like Merv around

to mix your chocolate milk?" she asked, stepping into the double-story, marble-decked foyer that smelled of money.

"I did."

"Must be nice."

He laughed. "Still trying to guilt me out?"

"Just saying…"

"Merv does a great job. In return he is paid extremely well."

She pinned up a smile. "Then everyone's happy."

Jack must have been six-two or -three. In peep-toe flats that matched her simple white summer dress, Becca felt way less than her average height. When his scent filled her lungs, she fought the absurd urge to wither against him…even drag her lips all over those pecs. His chest was that good.

Before he shut the door, he did a double-take at her ride parked in the forecourt. "Tell me that's not a company car."

"My '63 Fiat Bambino is what's known as a true classic."

He squinted, looking harder—admiring the distinctive light mint-green shade, perhaps. "Are those dinky wheels even roadworthy?"

"I'm pretty sure it'll get us where we need to go."

He gave her a doubtful look. "*Pretty* sure."

"Are you ready?"

He shut the door and set his hands on the band of his jeans. She fought the urge to fan herself. She'd seen that body before, on a billboard advertising men's underwear.

"Ready to go where?" he asked.

"First of all," she pointed out, "you'll need clothes." *Or I'll go insane.* "Three to four changes."

"Sounds interesting."

"Oh, it will be."

With anticipation gleaming in his eyes, he nudged his

chin toward the stairs. "Come up while I pack. I might need further instruction."

As he headed off, Becca hesitated. But it wasn't as if he planned to throw her down on his bed and manacle her wrists to the posts. He wasn't that depraved. At least, she didn't think he was.

Steeling herself, she jogged up the stairs behind him.

"You didn't say where you're taking me," he said over one beautiful broad shoulder.

"On an adventure." *A journey.*

"Should I let anyone know?"

"Anyone, as in Angelica Lassiter?"

"She needs my support, now more than ever."

Becca's stomach pitched and she groaned. "God, I feel for her. I really do."

"But not enough to side with her."

"You know the answer to that."

At the top of the stairs, he turned left down a wide corridor. Examining the mouthwatering way his muscled back tapered to the incredible seat of those jeans, she kept close.

"Here's an idea," he said. "While you're trying to convince me to step back from a takeover, I could try to convince you to come join the dark side."

Join Jack Reed? *Ha!*

"I'm not the least drawn to the dark side."

He waited for her to catch up before continuing. "Not even a little bit?"

"Not even the teensiest baby thimbleful."

"Nothing in this world is simply black or white, you know."

She refrained from rolling her eyes. "Just pack, Jack."

They crossed a double threshold into a massive private suite. In this separate sitting room, blue brocade couches offered luxurious seating. Shelves filled with tomes lined an entire wall. An uneven pile of books lay stacked on an otherwise tidy desk. The room smelled of sandalwood. Masculine, soothing and unsurprisingly arousing.

Jack moved into an adjoining suite—the master bedroom. Becca took a calming breath and stayed precisely where she was.

"Will I need a dinner suit?" he called out while she ran a fingertip over book spines. Business, philosophy, a number of classics. One entitled *The Witchery of Archery*.

"No suit," she called back. "It'll be easy living all the way."

She moved to check out what was hung inside a large glass casing on a neighboring wall. "This bow looks like it belongs in a museum," she said loud enough for him to hear.

His deep disconnected voice filtered out from the bedroom. "It's thousands of years old, found preserved in ice in Norwegian mountains. The bow is made of elm. The arrow tip's slate. I won't say what I had to do to get hold of it."

She felt her eyes bulge. *Wow.* "This really does belong in a museum."

"I've had offers."

She took in the authentic Persian rug a few feet away. "Don't need the money, right?"

"It's not about money."

"It never is," she muttered, "when you eat caviar five days a week."

He went on, "It's about pride. It's about passion. A person should never give those away."

Passion… Becca peered out the window over his home archery field.

"So, have you ever split an arrow down the middle?" she asked, strolling over toward the view. "You know, like in the movies."

"That's a one-in-ten-thousand shot."

"So, that would be no?" she teased.

"I'm pretty good with apples though."

"On heads?"

"Just call me William Tell."

"I was thinking more Robin Hood, in reverse. Robbing from the poor to give to the rich."

"What about the theory that Robin Hood was nothing more than an outlaw?"

"In that case, I have the bases covered."

He emerged from the bedroom looking edible in a black polo shirt and tailored dark pants. Overnighter in hand, a wry smile on his face, he sauntered over.

"So now I'm a thief?"

"There is that theory," she said, "yeah."

As he lowered the case to the floor, his face came closer until the tip of his nose very nearly met hers. A tingling wave washed through her before settling in her chest.

"You're not worried that while we're away I might steal another kiss?" he asked close enough for his breath to brush her mouth.

Her suddenly sensitive nipples pushed against the lace cups of her bra. But now that she knew what to expect—knew just how to play this—it was within her power to resist.

She crossed her arms. "Like I said. Zip chance of defecting to the dark side."

While they were away, Becca planned to remind herself of that every minute of every day.

Five

Becca steered her Bambino north up Highway 1, tawny-colored hills on one side, awesome ocean bluffs and beaches on the other. With the windows rolled down, breathing in sweet oleander-scented air, she suggested that they play "Did you know?"

"Did you know," she began, "that there are no deaf birds or fish?"

Jack's dark hair ruffled around the sunglasses parked on his head. "I did *not* know that," he said, sounding suitably impressed.

"Did you know that one in every three hundred and fifty babies born have permanent hearing problems? Until twenty years ago, most children born with hearing problems weren't detected until they were two to three years of age. Now ninety-five percent of newborns are screened."

"That's good to hear." His grin was kick-ass sexy. "No pun intended."

After steering through a stomach-dropping curve, she

flicked over another look. Elbow hitched on the window ledge, foot tapping to 104 on the radio dial, Jack looked relaxed. Becca was stoked that he'd gone for this road trip idea even if it was simply because he needed the break from his desk. Of course, she knew Jack hadn't got to the top of his game by slacking off. No doubt he hoped this trip would be in some way beneficial, either by garnering information from her that might help advance his and Angelica's takeover plans, or by believing that he might actually pull off taking her to bed.

If she'd shared this smoldering chemistry with any other man, Becca might well have acquiesced. All kinds of sparks zapped around the room whenever she and Jack were together. But this week was not about romance. Definitely not about sex. It was about persuading a ruthless rich man not to add Lassiter Media to his wall of trophies. Becca wanted to reach Jack Reed's more human and merciful side. She wanted to help him accept that true pride came with peace of mind and compassion, not suffocating wealth and majority indifference.

Jack needed to find himself, and she was going to help shine the light. She'd started by planting him in the audience at a high school, making him a part of the swirl and the thrust. This morning she would introduce him to another foundation-funded scheme, as well as a person who had returned from the brink of despair to get her life back.

Later, Becca aimed to completely remove Jack from his cutthroat corporate element. She wanted to strip his defenses bare, make him forget who he was while nurturing his higher self. She had to believe there was some part of Jack Reed who would connect with the joys and importance of simple things, and also recognize that others less fortunate needed help to achieve even that connection.

She was excited about the little friend she had lined up for that part of their journey. Becca's friend, the owner of a gorgeous little dog, had come up with the idea. Chichi's antics could soften the hardest of hearts.

"Auditory areas of the brain," Becca went on now, "are most active not only when a child listens but also when he reads. Isn't that amazing?"

"How's your foundation involved?"

"It isn't *my* foundation. Not really."

"But the dream is to head your own charity someday?"

"If I did, it'd help all kinds of causes, like Lassiter's foundation does. I couldn't choose just one."

"If you had to?"

Concentrating on the snaking road, Becca ran through worthy causes in her mind.

"I'd want to give hope to homeless kids," she finally said. "I spent time in foster care." She pulled up in her seat and then took another sweeping turn. "I lucked out with my last family."

"The one with the bakery."

Ah... The smell of freshly baked bread and cinnamon-apple fritters in the morning. By then, she had felt transported to heaven.

"It was the first time and place I remember ever feeling truly safe. And loved." Such a beautiful, warm, *vital* feeling. "I was eleven, the age when a kid starts to mature, to change…when we question everything three times over and still have more to ask. But my parents seemed to have all the answers."

"How'd they manage that?"

"With patience and kindness. Plenty of communication. Talking. But mainly listening."

"Which brings us back to *did you know*."

She smiled. *Right*. "Did you know that the foundation is helping fund clinical trials of auditory brainstem implants in children?"

"You're really into kids."

"We all started out as one."

When he didn't reply, she glanced across again. He was studying the ocean. A pulse popped steadily above his jaw. Had she made him truly think or was she simply boring his pants off? Not that she needed that image in her head. It was tough enough battling the epic visual of his bare chest and arms when he'd opened his front door earlier that day. The memory alone made her breath come short.

"I got one for you," he said suddenly.

"One what?"

"A did you know."

Cool. "Shoot."

"Did you know, once a long time ago, I almost got married?"

Becca's grip on the wheel slipped and the Bambino swerved before she corrected and got back onto their side of the road. She pushed out a shaky breath.

"Jesus, Jack, don't throw those curveballs while I'm driving."

Jack Reed's reputation as a corporate raider was trumped only by his name as a player. He was always on the hunt for something or someone to jump into bed with, before moving on to some other project.

Seriously. *Marriage?*

"So…what happened?" She smirked. "Did she break your heart?"

"In a sense. She died."

Gravel sprayed as the car veered onto the shoulder. Was this a bad joke? Given the tight line of his mouth, she guessed not.

"Jack…" *God.* "I'm sorry."

"Like I said. It was a long time ago. A *lifetime* ago." His gaze sharpened on hers as his eyebrows knitted together. "You okay?"

"I just…wasn't expecting that."

Not for one minute.

He studied her white-knuckled grip on the steering wheel. "Want me to drive?"

"That could work." He might even enjoy it. "Except… this clutch slips a bit. The steering wheel wobbles a lot of the time. She's a temperamental beast."

"But full of heart."

Exactly. "I think she's worth the trouble."

When she looked across, Jack's thoughtful gaze probed hers. "I was thinking the same thing."

Becca parked the *antique-mobile* out front of a redbrick single-story building. With its barred, round-arch windows, it was a cross between last-century public housing and urban old-English church.

During the rest of the drive, they'd spoken more about charities, including the fact that J.D. had left a good deal of cash to the Lassiter Charity Foundation. That segued into a discussion that touched upon the recent grand opening of the Lassiter Grill in Cheyenne. Jack had attended the opening with Angelica, which hadn't gone down so well with the Lassiter "in" crowd. He mentioned that he hadn't been invited to Dylan's wedding to Jenna Montgomery; it had been very much a family-only affair.

Becca had then trilled about Felicity Sinclair's upcoming nuptials to Chance Lassiter. Jack couldn't see himself being invited to that shindig, either.

Now, as he and Becca walked up the rickety cement-block path, Jack pushed that other business aside to focus on a neat rainbow painted over the building's entrance.

He scratched his chin. "Are we here to listen to a sermon?"

Becca reached back to release her ponytail and shake it out. "We're here to test your powers of observation."

Like observing how her hair unraveled around her

shoulders like spools of gold silk? The way her every gesture and expression carried the conviction of what she believed in? Above all else, Becca believed in herself—what she was about and why.

She resembled Jack in that regard.

Not that he needed to explain himself to anyone—not for any reason. Although, when they'd played that game earlier in the car, he had given in to the impulse to throw a private snippet out there: if Krystal hadn't died, they would have been married. Things would have been different.

Jack rarely thought about that period of his life. It stirred up unpleasant feelings, doubts, memories—well, obviously.

"How would you rate yourself?" Becca asked. "On observation."

"I see what I need to see."

"What you *want* to see."

His gaze skimmed her lips. "That, too."

He swung open the front glass door and they crossed to a counter. A vase of marigolds sat at one end, a framed headshot announcing "Employee of the Month—Brightside House" on the other. Becca addressed the receptionist.

"Hi, Torielle. Mind if I take a guest through?"

The woman had a magic smile, the type that made a person want to beam back. "You know you're welcome here anytime, Becca. Anytime at all."

"Torielle Williams, this is Jack Reed."

Torielle's dark-chocolate gaze flickered—perhaps she recognized the name and its recent connection to the Lassiter scandal in the media. But her smile didn't waver.

"Pleased to meet you, Mr. Reed. Let me know if there's anything you need."

As they headed down a corridor, Jack felt Becca's energy swell and glow. She was a natural leader, a person who got the job done. Knowing she was out for his scalp would have upset a lesser opponent. Instead Jack found himself absorbing her spirit. What might they accomplish if Becca and he sat on the same team?

"This facility helps long-term unemployed women not only find work but also regain their self-esteem," she said. "No matter the color, creed, age or background, we do whatever needs to be done to get them back into contributing, earning and growing as individuals."

They stopped at a window that opened onto another room. Inside, a group was immersed in doing nails and makeup. Numerous rails of women's clothing were lined neatly off to one side.

"Every obstacle is tackled," Becca said, "from grooming and carriage to interview skills and continuing education."

Jack stole a look at Becca's hands resting on the window ledge. Her nails were cut short, no polish. Her makeup was minimal, too, if she wore any at all. Her kind of bone structure and flawless skin didn't need any help. Good diet, plenty of uninterrupted sleep. Jack imaged her opening her eyes each morning and bouncing out of bed. He usually hit the snooze button at least twice. Insomnia was a bitch.

Farther on, they stopped at another window and saw a well-dressed woman addressing a room full of women who were taking notes. Then the next room was a gym. Exercise classes were in full swing—spin bikes, Pilates, ball games.

"Everyone's enjoying themselves," he said.

"Exercise releases endorphins. Feeling good is addictive, Jack." Her shoulder nudged his arm. "You got to keep it pumping."

Jack grinned. "You like to push yourself."

"That's the way to success."

"As long as you don't burn out."

"No chance of that when you're doing what you love."

"And you love what you're doing."

"Every minute."

"Even troubleshooting problems like me?"

They faced each other and she tilted her head, as if she were trying to see him more clearly—see the good.

"You, Jack, are a challenge."

"But redeemable?"

"Everyone's redeemable." Her fingers tapped his shirt-front. "Even you."

Next was a stop at a newer facility separate from the main building. Groups of young children were painting, playing dress-up, making mud pies. Minders were engrossed in helping, sharing, laughing.

"A child-care facility?" he asked.

"And after-school facilities with a bus service to deliver and collect the kids. There's a nursery for the newborns, too."

As they walked along a fence lined with fragrant yellow flowers, Becca explained.

"In the States, more women than men are poor, and the poverty gap is wider here than anywhere in the Western world. When parents separate or divorce it's more likely that mothers will take on the financial responsibilities of raising the kids. Childcare costs can be crippling, never mind medical expenses. While we get a woman prepared to interview for jobs, we make certain any children are properly supervised and cared for."

A little girl with pink track shoes and big brown eyes saw Becca and waved her paintbrush hello over her head. Becca waved back and blew her a kiss before leading Jack back into the main building.

"Who was that?" he asked.

"Wait a minute and I'll let you guess."

They entered a room. Women sitting at half a dozen computer workstations glanced up and greeted them both.

Becca sat at a vacant desk and logged in while Jack stood behind her, attention on the computer screen. She opened up a file labeled "Before." There were countless entries, each catalogued by a headshot.

"These are just some of the women who the facility has helped," she said, enlarging a "Before" image. Not only did the woman look disheveled, her resigned expression said she'd accepted that disappointment was her lot in life.

"She never finished high school," Becca said, studying the screen. "For years she suffered in a domestic violence situation. Her husband put her in hospital more than once but she never pressed charges because she feared the next beating would be worse. Her teeth were broken. Can you imagine the agony of feeling discriminated against because of your smile? She was living in a shelter with her children when she came to us."

"Did she get a job?"

From her seat, Becca grinned up at him. "You don't recognize her?"

"No." Then he blinked, focused harder. "Wait…" Something in those eyes… "Torielle?"

"Just two years ago."

Of course. "The receptionist with the dynamite smile."

"We have several professionals, including dentists, who donate their time. Now Torielle helps out here part-time and is working toward completing a college degree."

"And the girl waving her paintbrush, saying hello…?"

"Chelsea, Torielle's four-year-old daughter. She has two older brothers in grade school, twins. The boys both want to become jet pilots. They're smart enough, too. Chelsea wants to be a ballerina—every little girl's dream, and why not?"

"A happy ending," Jack said as Becca clicked to Torielle's "After" picture. The difference, the pride—real pride—shone from the inside out.

"We want to set these facilities up all over the country," Becca said.

"But they need ongoing support."

"The way we see it, we give a little now and society gets a whole lot back later."

Becca pushed to her feet and smiled into his eyes, a beautiful smile Jack had seen before but not as clearly as he did this minute. Becca was one of those uniquely special individuals who bobbed up every now and then. Unselfish, exuberant. She was physically attractive but it was her attitude that made everything about her shine...even when she was chewing someone out.

"Are you ready for a change of pace?" she asked.

His gaze swept over her silken waves of hair. "What do you have in mind?"

"Something different." She winked. "Something fun."

Six

"My God. What the hell *is* that?"

Frowning at Jack's remark, Becca crossed over to the small, seemingly unsupervised dog. "You're lucky he's not sensitive," she said.

They had driven from Brightside House a short distance to a small, quiet parking lot located this side of a beach. When they'd gotten out of the car, this little guy had been waiting alone as planned. Chichi would play a role in Becca's weeklong challenge. Her overriding strategy was to reach Jack's more human, less sophisticated side. He couldn't help but lower his defenses with this cute dog around.

For the next two days of her remaining six, she would hide Jack away from all the temptations and reminders that drove his *conquer and take all* mentality. He needed to get back to basics, and appreciate that everyone deserved a chance to achieve at least that, too.

Now, studying the dog, Jack visibly shuddered. "Sorry, but that's got to be the ugliest mutt I've ever seen."

"Haven't you heard?" Crouching, Becca stroked the wispy tuft of hair on the dog's head. "Beauty is skin deep."

"Except when ninety-five percent of the skin is bald and dappled—" he shuddered again "—and please, not scaly, too."

"He's a Chinese-crested Chihuahua mix."

"If you say so." He flipped a finger at its head. "Do you think its tongue always lolls out the side of its mouth like that?"

She dropped a kiss between the puppy's ears. "Cute, huh?"

"God as my witness, I've never seen anything like it."

"Chichi will be joining us on our road trip."

Jack's head went back. "You know this dog?" As if to answer for her, Chichi sneezed and Jack shrank back. "Whatever it's got, let's hope it's not contagious. Does he smell?"

"Not as well as a bloodhound."

"That's not what I meant."

As she ran a palm down Chichi's hairless back, his pink tongue lolled out more. "Did you have a dog growing up?"

"Would it be too unkind to suggest those bobble eyes look possessed?"

"Jack?" *Focus.* "Growing up?"

"Yeah. We had a King Charles."

"To go with the thoroughbreds, right?"

Chichi's skinny tail with its pompom tip whipped the sandy ground; he got the joke.

Becca pushed to her feet. "He wants you to pick him up."

Jack crossed his arms and puffed out his chest. "You pick him up."

"That's pathetic."

Jack hashed it out some more and finally exhaled. He edged forward, gingerly hunkered down and scooped the dog up. Chichi's eyes grew heavy, contented, looking up into his. "Are you running some kind of weird dog make-over campaign?"

"We all need to be loved."

Jack shot her a look. "You're not trying to get me to adopt this thing, are you? Because my lifestyle isn't con-ducive, to say the least."

"He's on loan from a friend." The longtime owner of the café right next to this parking lot.

As Chichi's head and tongue craned up, Jack recoiled. "And the friend wants it back?"

"Oh, c'mon. You're not that harsh."

He arched a brow. "I have it on good authority that I am."

From many, including Becca. And yet Jack must have owned a soul at some point. He'd wanted to marry that woman, hadn't he? Ipso facto, he'd been in love, a self-sacrificing condition from all accounts. Of course, he could've simply been trying to screw with her brain. She wouldn't put it past him. And yet somehow, deep down, Becca knew he'd told the truth, at least about that.

Still gazing up at Jack, Chichi put his miniature paw on his chest. What a picture.

"He's really taken to you," she said.

The dog yipped and one side of Jack's mouth twitched— almost a grin. "He sounds like a mouse."

Moving closer, Becca ran a palm over Chichi's head. When the dog laid his ear against Jack's chest, her fingers skimmed that solid warmth, too, and for one drugging moment she imagined herself curled up in those capable arms, snuggling in against that sensational rock of a chest.

"He loves the sand and water," she said.

"That's my cue to take him for a walk while music plays over a slow-motion montage."

"I'm not aiming that high." Yet. She did, however, want to bring out Jack's softer, more compassionate side.

When Jack set him on the ground, Chichi trotted off down the wooden-slat path to the beach. Then he stopped and looked back, as if making sure he was being followed.

Shielding his gaze from the sun, Jack surveyed the quiet area. "We'll need a leash."

"It's a leash-free beach."

"So a bigger dog can just romp up and have him for lunch?"

"Hasn't happened yet."

"A hawk might swoop and carry him off. I'm *serious*."

Becca was laughing. Was Jack embarrassed or just being difficult? Either way, she was going to win. She skirted around the rear to give him a good push. But when she set her palms on his back, ready to shove, heat swirled up her arms, zapping her blood all the way to her core. At the same time, Jack spun around and, playing, caught her hands.

She should have stepped back then and put some physical distance between them. But his expression changed so quickly from games to that intense, dark gaze searching hers…when a thick vein in his throat began to throb, she couldn't help it. Becca felt mesmerized by the beat.

Chichi's yip broke the trance. The sound of waves washing onto shore faded back up. Again, she felt wind pulling through her hair. Light-headed, she edged back at the same time Jack reached to bring her closer. He missed catching her by a whisker.

Gathering herself, Becca nodded toward Chichi. "Go on," she said in an unintentionally husky voice. "He's waiting."

"What about you?"

"I have someone to see." Her friend, Chichi's owner.

He took two purposeful steps, closing the gap between them again. Had he suddenly grown six inches? Becca felt dwarfed…very nearly consumed.

"Becca, you said this was fun time."

Her heart was pounding so hard, she had to swallow against the knot lodged in her throat before tacking up a smile.

"So…" She shrugged. *"Have fun."*

But Jack didn't move. If he reached for her hand now, Becca wasn't sure which way it might go. How easy would it be to pretend they were a regular couple out for the day with their dog on the beach. But this wasn't about her. Definitely wasn't about them *as a couple.*

The intensity in Jack's expression finally eased. When he bent to slip off his shoes, Becca released that breath. As he trotted off down onto the beach, Chichi scampered back up, trying to scoot between his legs on each step. When Jack almost stumbled, Becca laughed. Glancing back, he laughed, too—a hearty, deeply stirring sound that in some ways touched Becca's heart.

She had to believe…

There must be hope for us all.

Amidst a clump of dried seaweed, Jack found a stick to toss while Becca disappeared in through the front door of a café located next to the parking lot. When what's-his-face let out a bark, Jack refocused and hurled the stick toward the water. He watched the dog scamper off, kicking up sand as he went. It was a perfect Californian day, Jack was a fan of the beach and, okay, this dog was half-cute in a sincerely *off* kind of way. But Jack's mind was stuck on Becca. First, he understood the visit to Brightside House. Becca had wanted to bring him up close and personal with the good work her foundation was doing, the real life people the funds helped. The way she had highlighted Tori-elle's dramatic change in circumstances had been a nice touch. It was obviously a worthwhile and solid program.

But what was she thinking lumping him with a dog? Was this introduction somehow linked to opening his eyes in connection to a pet adoption agency, perhaps? What-ever Becca was hatching here had to do with advancing her cause of coaxing him away from a takeover bid.

She would be pleased to hear that this morning had made him think.

More importantly, Becca made him *feel*. Whenever they touched, even a brush, Jack felt it to the marrow of his bones—they had sexual compatibility through the roof. And a minute ago, he'd put a finger on at least one reason for that. Becca wasn't *playing* hard to get. She *was* hard to get. It wasn't happening, not in this lifetime, even while they both felt temptation gnawing and growing between them. With Becca, ethics came first, last and everywhere in between.

If they should happen to come to some understanding regarding the rescue of her beloved foundation, she would worry that a rogue like him could always go back on his word. She might suggest a contract with special clauses, Jack supposed…in which case, perhaps he could slip in a couple of special private conditions of his own.

Nah. That was low, even for him.

Jack was between throws and watching Becca from a distance as she spoke with a woman on the veranda of the café when his cell phone rang. After checking the caller ID, he pressed the phone to his ear.

"Angelica just called," Logan said. "She wanted my opinion again."

"And you said?"

Logan recited his standard response. "She needs to ac-cept the terms of the will."

"But she resisted."

"She still can't believe J.D. would do this to her. She's convinced there's some kind of conspiracy going on."

Jack transferred the cell to his other hand and tossed the stick again. "Poor kid."

"Angelica's hardly a child."

"There's a part of me that still sees her that way."

Jack had felt for Angelica having grown up without her mother, although from all reports her aunt had done a great job as a substitute. J.D.'s longtime widowed sister-in-law, Marlene, still resided in a private wing of the homestead belonging to the Big Blue.

Of course, her son, Chance, had inherited a whopping sixty percent of the ranch. Real generous of J.D. It must have made Angelica wonder if what appeared to be favoritism was gender-related. It made Jack wonder, too. If J.D. had sired a son rather than a daughter, would he have structured his will differently, leaving out the complications that Angelica was experiencing now?

Jack hadn't thought about being a father himself, not since he'd been in love with Krystal back in college. He'd been a different person then. His own most recent will left everything to Sylvia and some friends as well as to charity.

Ha. Wouldn't that make Becca's day.

Chichi was dancing on his hind legs, tongue flapping, wanting to play *fetch* some more.

"I'm away from the office the rest of the week," Jack told Logan, throwing the slimy stick yet again. Logan didn't need to know why he was away. The attorney was tetchy enough about this final stretch as it was.

"But you'll keep your cell on," Logan said.

"Angelica knows I'm available to talk day or night."

"And if she wants to speak face-to-face?"

"I'm there. No question."

A pause. "Maybe it would be better if you *weren't* available for a while."

"Can't do that, Logan. We agreed to play by the rules."

"Yeah." He exhaled. "I know."

When Jack caught sight of Becca leaving the café and heading down toward the entrance to the beach, he signed off.

Becca joined him on the sand a couple of minutes later.

"You were on the phone," she said. "Business?"

"Always."

"Nothing too urgent?"

"It's in hand." He glanced at the café. "I was hoping you might bring back supplies."

"What about you, Chichi?" Becca asked, bending and patting her thighs. "Hungry, little fella?"

The dog sneezed and barked and then picked up the stick and dropped it at Jack's feet again.

"His batteries don't wind down," he told Becca. "I've tossed that stick a hundred times."

"A hundred?"

"Definitely fifty."

"So, you've got those endorphins pumping?"

As a sea breeze picked up, pulling her summer dress back against the curves and valleys of her body, Jack nodded. "You could say I'm pumped, yeah."

She waved for them both to follow. As Jack jogged after her, he glanced over a shoulder. Chichi was sitting, stuck beside that stupid stick. Jack whistled through his fingers.

"Yo. Get a move on, slowpoke."

Chichi scampered up and damned if he didn't leap into Jack's arms like a circus act. Jack pulled his head away from that feral tongue and then caught up with Becca.

"So, tell me about the foundation's link to animal shelters." If that's what this was about.

"No links to shelters. I simply thought that while we

were here you two could meet," she said innocently as she collected Jack's loafers because his hands were full. "Pets are good for humans."

"So are other humans."

"Yep. Having friends is important."

"What would you say to you and me becoming friends?"

She gave a small smile. "Oh, Jack, you know that's not possible."

"But it *would* be possible if I backed away from Lassiter Media?"

A glimmer of hope lit her eyes. "That sure would be a start."

As they walked up to the café, Jack ran over that last bit of conversation in his mind. If he were to spend time with Becca outside of this current context, he would have preferred to tick the "sex between consulting adults" box. And yet he had asked about them becoming *friends? And* he'd meant it. Clearly he had left off the "with benefits" part.

Jack was reading the name on the café's facade, *Hailey's Favorite Haunt,* when a van rolled up alongside the Bambino; the insignia of a top-rating tabloid entertainment news show was stenciled on the side. Jack's antennae twitched. Over the years, he'd tackled his fair share of reporters—truckloads since word of his possible takeover bid for Lassiter Media had leaked. But that crew wasn't here to hassle him. Normally he planned every minute of his day, from first call in the morning to final perusal of documents at night. However, Becca had drawn up this itinerary. No one knew he was here, not even Sylvia. The crew had probably pulled up to grab a coffee for the road.

Then a man jumped out the side door of the vehicle with a camera perched on his shoulder, and Jack paused. Next, a well-dressed woman with a mic climbed out the front passenger side, immediately focused on him and smiled like he was expecting her. Jack set his jaw.

Was this ambush somehow a part of Becca's weeklong deal? If so, he was not amused.

Seven

On their way up to the café, Becca heard someone call out Jack's name. She stopped to track down the source. A tall, slender woman in a bright tangerine skirt-suit and a man with a news camera balanced on one shoulder were ambling across the parking lot, headed their way.

An ice-cold feeling cut through her middle. No one other than her friend had known to expect her at this time. So what was a tabloid TV crew doing here? And what kind of spin would they put on her presence here with Jack?

Holding Chichi close, Jack asked, "Know anything about this?"

She shook her head.

"Lord knows how they'll twist this."

Jack growled. "God, I hate the media."

Becca's hackles went up. "You did happen to notice the name of the company you want to take over, didn't you? Lassiter *Media*. Not that you intend to keep it long." Keep it *whole*.

He repositioned Chichi against his chest. "We can be chewing each other out when that reporter reaches us or we can feed her crumbs and hopefully they'll slouch off."

The reporter and her cameraman were seconds away. Becca exhaled. "Any idea what crumbs?"

A wicked grin eased across his face. "I have a couple in mind."

"Mr. Reed, isn't it?" the reporter asked when she reached them. "Jack Reed. And you're Becca Stevens, head of the Lassiter Charity Foundation. Do you have a moment to answer a few questions?"

Jack replied for them both. "No trouble at all."

"Mr. Reed, you're aware of the publicity and unrest surrounding speculation that you and Angelica Lassiter may succeed in a takeover bid of Lassiter Media after she was shut out of running the company. Would you care to comment on this secluded get-together between yourself and a respected member of Evan McCain's umbrella management team?"

"Ms. Stevens and I have business to discuss regarding the foundation," Jack replied.

The reporter cocked her head and then made a point of eying Jack's loafers, which Becca still held.

"A leisurely day at the beach seems an odd way to discuss business," she said. "Could this be viewed more as a date? And if so, Ms. Stevens, how will you explain this kind of rendezvous to your Lassiter colleagues who are pretty down on Mr. Reed at the moment?"

Becca's blood pressure spiked. This might not look kosher at first glance, but her colleagues would never believe that she'd turned Benedict Arnold. They knew where her heart lay and it was not with Jack Reed.

"As Mr. Reed explained," she replied with barely a tremor in her voice, "today is strictly business."

The reporter's sky-blue eyes narrowed to slits. "So the

rumors regarding a romantic liaison between the two of you are unfounded?"

That hit her in the chest. *"What the—?"*

"My sole purpose today," Jack replied, "is to build on my already solid support of the Lassiter Charity Foundation. Now, we're late for an appointment. I'll thank you both to leave us to our privacy."

Becca rubbed a throbbing temple. She'd never suffered from migraines but she was sure she was getting one now.

How would Evan McCain react if or when this hit the airwaves? She had wanted to keep quiet about her long shot plan to crack Jack's enigmatic side and in some way at least sway his thinking. Now she would need to contact Sarah, her assistant, as well as Evan, to reassure them that she hadn't shifted camps, and never would.

Or maybe it would be wiser to simply call this all off now.

After Jack set Chichi down, Becca led him around the café's wide veranda to an ocean-facing table set with a reserved sign.

"You realize the dog has followed us," Jack said quietly, casting glances at the other guests sprinkled inside the café as well as out here in the fresh air.

"No problem," Becca said. "Trust me."

They were taking their seats when Becca's friend appeared in her trademark denim skirt and vest. They'd had a conversation earlier at this very table when she'd left Jack on the beach.

"Jack Reed," Becca said, "meet Hailey Lang."

"Pleased to meet you," Hailey said with the hint of a Texas twang. Her family had moved over from Houston twenty years ago when Hailey was eight. "I saw you tripped up by some pesky reporter."

"They appeared out of nowhere," Becca said, and then

noticed how Hailey averted her gaze before she spoke again, upbeat this time.

"How you doing there, Chichi?"

Now Jack looked between the dog and Hailey. "You know each other, too?"

"He's my baby," Hailey said while Chichi sat patiently by her feet, his tail fanning the wood planking. "He's a bit of a celeb around these parts."

Jack leaned back in his chair. "He does kind of grow on you."

"So, Chichi's going on a trip with you guys. One of his favorite things is riding shotgun."

"He's partial to sticks, too. Which reminds me…" Jack got to his feet. "If you'll excuse me, I need to wash up before lunch."

As Jack moved off, Hailey crouched down beside Becca's chair. "Becca, honey, I think I might need to apologize."

"For reserving us the best table in the house?"

"The reporter who gave you grief just now…" She leaned closer. "Thing is I have a regular who comes in most days around brunch time for our Delite Mushroom Omelet. Anita's daughter works for the same cable show. Anita talks about her all the time, how she's a hound, always after a big scoop. I think Anita overheard part of our conversation earlier about what you're doing here with Jack Reed. I think she tipped her daughter off."

Becca thought back. "You mean the redhead with a French twist, who was sitting a couple of tables over?" Becca had felt that woman's eyes on them a few times earlier.

"Anita McGraw has a keen ear for gossip. And if there's none around, she'll make dirt up." Hailey sighed. "Is it going to cause much trouble, hon?"

Nothing could be done about it now. And Becca didn't

want Hailey to feel responsible or to worry. "It'll be fine," she assured her friend as Jack returned to the table.

She would make those phone calls to Sarah and Evan's office. She'd decide then on whether or not to cancel this challenge.

Looking halfway relieved, Hailey pushed to her feet.

"Do I need a menu?" Jack asked, pulling his chair in. "I'm open to suggestions."

Hailey piped up. "Chef's salad and specialty pizza. That's with prosciutto, caramelized pear and goat cheese."

"I'm in," Becca said.

"Times two. So, how did you two become friends?" Jack asked, shaking out a napkin to place on his lap.

"Coming up two years ago, Becca broke down just over there, this side of the median strip." Hailey nodded toward a section of road. "Chichi let me know someone needed help. He zipped right up to me, turning circles like his tail was on fire."

"Water pump," Becca explained. "It'd been coughing all the way up the coast. The hood was spewing steam."

"I have a cousin just round the corner—the best mechanic in town," Hailey went on. "His specialty is old cars."

"*Classic* cars," Becca corrected. "He wanted to buy it, remember?"

"I sure do," Hailey said. "You wouldn't take the money even when he doubled the going rate. I don't *ever* see you giving up those wheels."

"There's no accounting for taste," Becca agreed. "Hailey ended up giving me a bed for the night while the repairs were done. Chichi slept at my feet."

Hailey sighed at Chichi, who was still gazing adoringly up at her. "That dog there is a fine judge of character."

Jack grinned. "And yet he likes me?"

"We were watching you two on the beach." Hailey winked at Jack. "He likes you a *whole* lot."

Becca had a moment of what psychologists term cognitive dissonance. She knew Chichi was a good gauge of character. She also knew he liked Jack. And yet Jack was not of good character. It made her brain hurt.

Hailey headed off. "I'll get this order under way and finish packing that ice chest for you all."

"Ice chest?" Jack asked, pouring water for them both from a carafe. "Are we going on a picnic?"

"Not a picnic, as such," Becca said and he grinned.

"Another one of your secret destinations?"

"With no chance of reporters this time." She lifted her glass. "One hundred percent guaranteed."

But first, she'd check with the boss.

Three hours later, watching out for media tails the whole way, Becca pulled the Bambino up in the middle of freaking nowhere—or, rather, somewhere east of Fresno.

Chichi was asleep on Jack's chest. The drool went from his neck to—he didn't want to think about it. With the dog's head and that tongue hanging out the window more than half the time, the car's side panel must be Slime City by now.

Jack surveyed the area. Dense woods. Lonely cabin. Cooler shadows creeping in.

"What is this?" he asked. "Boot camp?"

Becca jerked on the parking brake. "Actually…yeah."

While Becca got out of the car, Jack wondered how he could extricate himself without disturbing the dog. Which was crazy…except, with one leg kicking and eyelids twitching, the mutt looked like he was having a nice dream. When Becca opened the passenger side door, Chichi stirred, stretched and expelled a big smelly yawn. Then he jumped onto a carpet of pine needles and trotted off into the woods.

Becca was at the trunk. Jack eased out from the car and stretched out his own kinks, frowning as he watched the dog's cotton-top tail disappear among the trees.

"Aren't you worried about him?"

"Chichi's been here before," she said, handing over Jack's bag. "He knows his way around."

"Does he know his way around a mountain lion?"

"Don't forget the black bears and rattlesnakes."

She was screwing with him, but a chill rippled up Jack's spine just the same.

Heading for the door, she added, "He'll come the minute you call."

"If you're not worried, I'm not worried."

Jack grabbed the ice chest from the backseat and shut the door with a hip. "What did Hailey pack in here? Cement blocks?"

"Bread, fruit, cheese, refreshments—"

"Beer?"

"And wine."

They were most definitely set then. For what exactly, he had no idea.

"I got the high school visit and Brightside House. Forgive me if I sound slow, but what am I doing way the heck out here with a dog?"

"For two days and nights, I've kidnapped you," she said, heading for the front door. "Transported you away from your obsession with killer deals and accruing power so that you can get in touch with reality and learn some lessons on how to unleash your truer, less egocentric self."

"After which I will accept a higher calling and disavow my evil ways."

"*Ahh*…doesn't that sound heavenly?"

"It sounds like you're dreaming."

"Some of the world's biggest dreams have come true because someone believed and made others believe, too."

When a couple of huge examples came to mind, he couldn't argue the point. "And the mutt?"

"I knew he'd make you smile in a different way than you're used to."

"So, I'll change my mind about Lassiter Media because I played with a dog? Because I smiled differently?" *Come on.*

"Actions trigger emotions that link with the process of decision-making. I'm hoping that sometime this week, you'll not only smile differently, but start to *think* and choose differently, too."

Okay, fine. "Does Evan know about this cozy getaway?"

"He does now. I phoned him before we left the café. I didn't want him finding out from…other sources."

Like that tabloid show. "And he was okay with it?"

"He said he trusts my judgment and admires my determination."

"In that case, you get an A for creativity. Except you're forgetting one thing. Even when I want to, I never let emotions dictate my decisions."

Her expression didn't waver. "Then we'll simply call this a break from civilization."

Sure. Although he could do without the overgrown rat, he wouldn't object to hanging out here alone with this beautiful woman. Maybe he could put a spin on things and have *Becca* thinking differently by the time they left. And he wasn't talking business.

Inside, the place was quiet and dark enough at four in the afternoon to need to turn on the light. But Becca continued on from the front door without flicking a switch. Jack gave his eyes time to adjust. The room was sparsely furnished, no window dressings. Some walls were plastered. Others displayed exposed logs. It smelled like raccoons might have lodged in the cupboards over winter.

"Who owns this place? The foundation?"

He found Becca in a room that housed a double-bed covered with a patchwork quilt and matching pillows. A painting, featuring wilted poppies, hung above the headboard. Becca was setting her bag near a lopsided freestanding wardrobe.

"The cabin belongs to my parents," she said.

"When was it last used?" Jack sniffed the musty air. "1965?"

"Are you uncomfortable?" She faced him, hands on hips. "Out of your silver-spoon element?"

"Wasn't that the idea?"

With a wistful smile, she peered out the window at the trees. "We used to vacation here for a week every year. No television or hairdryers or—"

"Electricity?"

A camping lantern sat perched on top of a set of drawers. She flicked a switch and white light filled much of the space. "Ta-dah!"

Loving her bright smile, he moved closer. "Very rustic." He stopped before her, close enough to absorb the contentment and pride shining in her eyes. "Is there a second bedroom?"

"There is—complete with two sets of bunk beds, meant for kids, not a man of your sizable build."

His heart gave a running jump. "So, one bed?"

"And a cot." She nodded toward a corner. A saggy camper bed was tucked away among the shadows.

Oh. "Right." He scratched a temple. "That might work." *Not.*

"Guess we don't need to draw straws. I get the cot."

Jack growled as she moved across to inspect it. "Becca, I'm not letting you spend the night on that."

"Lots of people sleep on benches, in doorways, alleys, under bridges, in subways and behind Dumpsters—"

"Okay, okay." He'd heard enough. Guess her first point in bringing him here had been made. "I'll take the cot."

"You'll break it."

"If I do, I'll reimburse you." And see a chiropractor, end of discussion. "But it's a long way from lights-out. What do you have planned until then? Ghost stories around a campfire?"

Jack had a couple up his sleeve. She might even need two strong arms to help with the fright factor.

"A campfire?" she asked. "You mean outside with the bears and rattlesnakes?"

Jack paused. *Good point.*

"First we make the beds," she said. "Then a nice relaxing bath to wash off the travelers' dust."

An image of the two of them together caressing in a deep, sudsy hot tub faded up in his mind. Pure fantasy. Still, he didn't want to put a damper on her idea.

He rocked back on his heels. "Sounds good."

"Great. We'll need maybe ten buckets' full."

"Full of what?"

"Water. We don't exactly have a bath or a shower. We do, however, have a washtub."

Jack waited for the punch line.

His grin dropped.

She was serious.

"Aren't you going to let me know how many people go without adequate plumbing?"

"Don't need to. You worked it out yourself."

He grinned. *Lesson two: check.*

Becca moved to the drawers and found some sheets while he took his place on the other side of the bed. She fluffed out the lower sheet and proceeded to pull the elasticized end under the top corner of the mattress. He did the same on his side of the bed and then tackled the lower corner.

It was a cinch.

As she fluffed out the top sheet, she asked, "Ever made a bed before?"

He scoffed. "I'm sure I have."

"You'd have a housekeeper now, of course."

"Weekdays."

"How long has she worked for you? It's a woman, yes?"

"Mary's worked for me maybe four years."

"Long-time employee?"

"You could say that."

"So, Mary who?"

"Why do you want to know my housekeeper's last name?" What did that have to do with her plan to turn him around on the takeover question?

"I'm curious is all."

As they both stretched the sheet across the middle of the mattress, Jack searched his memory and came up a blank. "It'd be in my phone."

She moved to the end of the bed. "Uh-huh."

From across the mattress, Jack narrowed his eyes at her. "You know all your employees' names off the top of your head?"

"It's fine, Jack. Honest."

"Now you're patronizing me?"

"Is this you being defensive?"

"I'm more than happy with who I am."

She slipped her side of the sheet under the mattress. "Well, that's the main thing, isn't it."

"Why do I feel as if you just insulted me?" he asked, scooping under his end.

"You're smart enough to work it out."

"Just say I'm not."

She joined him on his side of the bed. "You live such a

privileged life, you take for granted clean sheets, and those who change them for you. Lots of children have to do their own laundry. Lots of people would do anything for any kind of bed to sleep on. Want to hear more."

He rubbed the back of his neck. "Not right now."

"Want to learn how to do a hospital corner then?"

Jack moved back to give her room. She bent to collect the dangling edge of the sheet and hold it out from the bed. Then she scooped the linen under the mattress and all the way up. At least he thought that's what she'd done. Call him a man, but even after the speech, Jack was more interested in the view of her legs and those buns.

Straightening, she turned to him. "Think you can do that?"

He feigned an uncertain look. "I might need help."

She moved back to her side, and nodded at the to-be-hospital-tucked bottom corner. "Go ahead. Have a go."

He crossed over and picked up the sheet at the wrong point.

"That's a little too far along," she said. "Let the sheet drop and naturally fold and try again."

He did as she instructed and then grabbed the sheet in a different spot.

"Here," she said patiently. "Like this."

She nudged in front of him and bent over again. Jack didn't see what happened next. He faintly heard some instructions. "...fold the lowest bit...smooth it under..." On autopilot, he moved in. His hand covered hers and they both tucked the sheet in.

"Like that?" he asked, close to her ear.

She didn't stiffen or jump away, so he closed his eyes and absorbed the moment. When she finally began to straighten, they disengaged and then simply stood there in the light and shadow, his hand holding hers as time ticked on and anticipation soared. When he coiled his arm around the front of her waist, he felt her intake of air. Pressing in behind her more, he imagined her biting her lip as she fought the urge to let nature take its course.

He brushed his lips over her temple, her cheek, all the while soaking up her scent. When he nuzzled her earlobe, he felt her quiver against him…heard her quiet, needful sigh. As he dragged his mouth down the side of her throat, bit by bit she tilted her head.

He nipped down the slope where neck met shoulder while his fingers left hers to skim the front of her dress. Through the cotton, he felt the start of her panties and, lower, the subtle rise of her mound. When she groaned— a low, wanting sound—half his blood supply rushed to a predetermined point.

"Jack…?" she murmured.

He hummed against her skin. *"Hmmm?"*

"The bed."

"What about the bed?"

"We were making it."

He dragged his grin back up to her ear. "I like making it with you."

When his fingers delved between her thighs, she made a husky noise in her throat that lit a fire in the pit of his belly. As his free hand slid up her side and under her breast, her head rocked back against his chest and her hand gripped his. Her voice was smoky now.

"This isn't what we're here for."

They were here to cut him off from reality and clobber him over the head with how little others had, how in need many of the less fortunate were.

"Okay." He nipped the side of her throat a little harder. "I'll stop."

When he didn't remove the hand between her legs, her grip over his tightened, not to drag him away but to hold his hand in place. His other palm dragged up over her breast and oh-so-lightly squeezed. She melted a moment before she pulled both his hands away and spun around. When she opened her mouth to speak, he got in first and lowered his head over hers.

Eight

When Jack pulled her close and his mouth captured hers, any objection Becca might have had dissolved like a teaspoon of sugar in hot water. As the kiss deepened, she reached to wind her arms around his neck. A moment more and she arched all the way in.

She would have denied it earlier, even to herself. The admission would have been incongruous, shameful. Inexcusable. She hadn't brought Jack here for this…and yet, secretly, Becca Stevens—the woman—had waited for this moment.

Now she couldn't think past the sensations sizzling through her system. Her breasts felt tender crushed against his chest. Suddenly her insides were filled with an emotion that felt like a swell of liquid fire.

Cupping her jaw, Jack held her mouth to his as he dropped back onto the bed, bringing Becca down along with him. Lips still locked, she tangled one leg around his and knotted her fingers in his clean dark hair while both his palms traced down her sides then slid over the rise of her behind.

Becca arched up and then ground down against him. Through their clothes she felt him already hard and ready. Reaching back, she clapped a hand over his where he was kneading the flesh above one thigh.

When he delved under her dress and down the back of her panties, a giant flash went off through her body. This all felt so new and necessary. So incredibly wrong and wonderfully right. She needed to get naked with Jack. She would *die* if she couldn't feel his hot skin on hers. She could barely breathe, the physical longing was so strong. So beautiful and bad and brilliantly intense.

As that first kiss broke down into hungry snatches, she wiggled to help him ditch her underwear. When he grabbed the hem of her dress and started to tug it over her head, she sat up and lifted her arms in the air. Straddled over his hips, her head back and eyes closed, she leaned in as he scooped her breasts out of their lace cups. His palms were big and hot and, dear heaven, just rough enough.

He was alternating between rolling and lightly plucking her nipples when she reached behind to unsnap her bra.

Her mistake was glancing down, seeing herself pretty much naked, thighs spread over a fully clothed man who, less than a week ago, she wouldn't have spat on let alone enjoyed mindless sex with.

Jack Reed. Number-one enemy…

What the hell am I thinking?

"I can't do this," Becca said, sweeping up the dress to cover what she could.

"Don't worry." He craned up to nuzzle her throat. "I'll guide you through."

"I mean this is a mistake."

His lips grazed her chin. "No mistake."

A hand curled around the side of her neck. Next she

knew, she was flipped onto her back and Jack was crouching, towering over her, unbuttoning his shirt, shrugging it off. His chest was so broad and bronzed, her fingertips tingled to sample every delicious mound and rung. When he maneuvered out of his pants and boxer shorts, she felt blood rush to her cheeks. This was moving much too fast.

He set a hand down next to her head. As one hot knee prized itself between hers, panic set in and both her hands shot out. She pushed against his pecs as he lowered himself onto her. A questioning look took hold in his eyes before he pulled slowly back and then frowned.

"You want to stop," he said—not a question, although the set of his mouth said it pained him to have to say it.

"One minute we were making the bed," she stammered. "The next…"

"You were kissing me."

"You kissed me!"

His grin flashed white. "You kissed me back."

She had. And, damn it, she wanted to kiss him again. Hard and deep and dirty. But this was wrong on so many levels, it made her head spin. And even if it were right…

Becca snatched a look down the length of his body and focused on that serious erection. As her heart pounded, she swallowed and then moistened her lips.

"Jack, we don't have protection."

"I have condoms."

"You do?" Wait. He *knew* this would happen?

"Better to be prepared than sorry," he pointed out.

Well, sure…except…it just reminded her how prepared Jack had been on so many other occasions. With so many other women.

She shook her head. *No.* "I can't do this."

"Do what?"

"This." She held her cheeks. "*Sex.* With you."

He hesitated and then, exhaling long and hard, he

brought her hand to his lips and tenderly kissed the palm. "I can't say I'm not bitterly disappointed," he murmured and then proceeded to kiss each fingertip.

Damn, he felt good, looked amazing, smelled divine. But even without the Lassiter complication, this was not a wise choice. Jack was a self-professed player. Sex was nothing more to him than sport. It meant as much as hitting a bull's-eye with an arrow.

While they'd been at the café, Becca had got away to make that phone call to Evan McCain. Then she'd explained the situation to her assistant. If the interview aired, she wanted everyone to know it was a beat up. But what would the world think if *this* ever got out?

She wiggled out from beneath him and set both feet on the floor. Avoiding his gaze, she put on her bra and shimmied back into her dress. It seemed that her panties, however, had disappeared. When she stood, she felt giddy… spacey…as if those last few moments had happened to somebody else on a distant planet.

Behind her, the bed squeaked; Jack had found his feet, too.

"I saw a lake when we drove in," he said as Becca listened to him shake out and then shrug back into his clothes. "I need to cool down and a washtub of water ain't gonna cut it."

He skirted around the bed, stood before her and then lifted her chin. His dark gaze was disappointed but also understanding.

"Why don't you come keep me company?"

Her stomach gave a kick and she found an excuse. "I should unpack…fix up this bed."

"Becca, I should warn you, if you say bed again in the next thirty seconds, I won't be held responsible for my actions."

Inside she shouted, *BED, BED, BED!*

Then she crossed her arms to stop herself from bringing him close.

"You go cool off," she said. "I'll be fine here."

He crossed to the bedroom door. "I'll find the mutt while I'm gone."

When she didn't reply, he kept going, through the main room and out the front door. Becca found her underwear, shoved her panties on and then sat on the side of the bed like a lump.

At the end of three solid minutes, her body was *still* vibrating—humming and smoldering with unruly heat. The unspent energy was driving her nuts! None of that was about to subside unless, or until, she did something about it.

She thought of the lake's cool mirrored surface, of swimming until she was too tired to move or so much as think about humping Jack Reed half the night. She made fists of her hands, tried to think rational thoughts. In the end, she grabbed two towels from the closet, her bikini from her bag and ran after Jack to catch up.

Becca got to the lake in time to see Jack cannonball off the pier and into the water. His clothes were hung on a branch near the bush she decided to hide behind. Waiting at the end of that pier, Chichi yipped, skidded forward and then jumped in, too.

That dog loved the water. Jack appeared to be a strong swimmer, too. He power-stroked a good length before flip-turning to head off in a different direction. He swam up to Chichi, who alternated between madly lapping at the water and barking excitedly. Treading water, Jack laughed, a sound that echoed across the lake, through the treetops and then down to wrap around Becca.

The water sure looked good. So did those dynamite arms and shoulders, that brilliant smile and slick dark brown hair. So good, in fact, Becca was forced to admit a truth.

Even if Jack Reed *was* a villain and these feelings were wrong and the world might shun her if anyone ever found out—there was no way around it. She liked Jack. She liked his smile and his wit. God help her, she liked his kiss.

Behind the bush, she changed into the bikini. When he started off again, swimming freestyle in the opposite direction, she darted down the pier, all the way to the end and, without stopping, dived into the deep.

Spearing through the cold water gave her a jolt, but, man, was it refreshing! Becca held her breath as long as she could. When she surfaced, Jack was right there, waiting not an arm's length away.

She yelped.

Chichi barked.

And Jack…well, he just grinned.

"How the hell did you do that?" she asked. He'd been at least ten yards away. Then it clicked. "You *knew* I followed you," she said, working hard to tread water.

"Bears make less noise."

"Why didn't you wait for me?"

"This was more fun."

Seriously? "Scaring me half out of my wits like that?"

"You weren't scared." As he waded closer, cool ripples lapped at her neck and chin. "You wanted to surprise me. I just turned it around."

He looked so relaxed and one step ahead of the game, she couldn't give it up that easily.

"I got to thinking that a swim would save filling up the washtub." When his smile spread, Becca tried to frown. "What's so funny?"

"You are." Although he'd be tall enough to stand at this depth, he began to paddle around her, his long, strong arms swerving inches beneath the surface. "Fess up. You wanted to come play."

He'd waded closer…near enough for Becca to reach out and touch.

"Maybe," she agreed. "This part of our week together is supposed to be about acknowledging your less complicated side. About seeing the bigger value in simple pleasures and understanding you can help bring them to others."

His smile changed again around the corners of his mouth. It was even sexier, more knowing. Mischievous and so hot.

But then he shook his head.

"What?" she asked, barely keeping her chin above the surface. Treading water, her limbs were feeling the burn now.

"I'm not doing it this time."

"Doing what?"

"You want me to sweep you over. You want me to kiss you. Only when we get started, you'll remember your higher purpose and make up some lame excuse why we ought to stop."

She objected to the one thing she could. "My excuses aren't lame."

He kept circling her, looking at her with that exasperating smile. He filled his mouth with water and squirted a fountain off to one side.

"Why don't you come over here?" he finally said.

Becca tried to stare him down but, in the end, she bit her lip and admitted, "This isn't very mature, is it?"

"Can we agree that we should be grown-up about the fact that we're attracted to each other?"

As he slid closer, she imagined his tongue rather than the water swirling over her belly, between her legs.

She nodded. *Damn it. Yes.*

"You know the consequences?" he asked.

She nodded again.

"And you still want this?"

Big breath. "Uh-huh."

Hot, strong fingers curled around her shoulders. Then their mouths joined and she was swept into the sublime haven of his arms.

He held her against his chest as their kiss played out—savoring, teasing, probing, until nothing else existed except the two of them and these sizzling, secret feelings.

When he broke the kiss, his lips stayed close. "Still okay?"

She rubbed her dreamy smile over his. "Okay isn't the word."

He tasted her lips again. "Wrap your legs around me."

She looped her arms around his neck and circled his hips with her legs, digging her heels in behind his thighs. He cupped her bottom and pulled her through the water, closer to him. As the length of his erection met the strip between her thighs, a jet of warm sparks flew through her veins. Her breath caught at the same time her head rocked back.

His hands slid under her behind. Then she felt his touch inside her bikini's crotch. His teeth dragged one half of her bikini top aside until the nipple was exposed and moist warmth covered that tip bobbing just above water level. While he drew that nipple back onto his tongue, his fingers slipped slowly up and down, over and between her folds. When his head pulled back a little and the edge of his teeth grazed her nipple, one finger slipped all the way inside of her.

She gasped, shuddered from top to toe, and then held his head in place against her breast.

The tip of his tongue rimmed the areola as he expertly massaged her down below. Every time his finger slid up, the tip grazed her G-spot, while one of his other fingers slipped up the outside, nudging the swollen bead hiding at the top of her folds. His pace was slow and steady, the perfect speed and pressure. Before long, she joined in with the rhythm, her hips rocking with his mesmerizing caress.

With each passing second, the sensations increased. As tingling heat ripped through her bloodstream, she needed to feel his mouth on hers again. She had to have him kissing her in a penetrating, all-or-nothing kind of way. Only the things his lips and teeth and tongue were doing added to the climb—a slope so steep, she had to gasp, the air was so thin.

When her orgasm broke, Becca curled into herself before she ground down against him and then released a cry that must have carried halfway to Montana. As she continued to shudder and groan, Jack watched a flow of raw emotions redefine her beautiful face. Holding her, loving her... This water might be chilly but he was rock-hard.

When he felt her floating down, he brought both his arms up around her waist to hold her against his chest. As her hot cheek nestled against the slope of his neck, he swirled her slowly through the water. Her ragged breathing gradually eased. Every now and then, her legs would twitch and then tighten around him again. He pressed a kiss to her crown, closed his eyes and wished every day could be as good as this.

After a few moments, she gave a big sigh, slid a palm over his shoulder and gradually lifted her face to his. Her smile was faraway. Satisfied. The loveliest smile he'd ever seen.

"You look like you could do with a nap," he joked.

"Are you kidding?" she asked groggily. "I may never let you sleep again."

Was she saying she wanted to do this every night? Jack could certainly arrange that. For a time, at least. Once they got back to the city, no doubt she would want to return to their former relationship…the one where she pretended to hate him.

She stretched her arms high over her head and then withered back against him, her lips landing on the pulse he felt beating at the side of his neck. The tip of her tongue tickled the spot.

"Hmm, you taste good," she murmured against his skin. "I want to taste every inch of you."

"Well, we're going to have to get out of the water for that."

She smiled up into his eyes. "Why?"

"A…we'll get all pruny. B…it's getting cold. C…something's nibbling at my toes and I don't need the distraction. D…"

"We don't have any protection," she finished.

Her dreamy gaze was growing clearer.

"We might have to shift camp, but look on the bright side," he said. "No one has to sleep on the cot."

Her legs tightened around him again. "I'll race you to shore."

"Okay, but I really don't think—"

Jack grunted as she used her feet against his abdomen to push off.

He let her have a head start and then sprang into action.

A moment later, when the water got too shallow for freestyle, he jumped up and stomped and splashed onto shore. Laughing and splashing too, she beat him by a nose. The prize was Jack crash-tackling her onto a patch of soft, long grass, working it so she landed on top of him, not vice versa. Then he rolled so she was pinned beneath him, his giggling prisoner.

In fact, Becca was laughing so much, she started to cough. He eased her up to a sitting position and patted her back. He didn't miss the fact that her body was even more sensational without all that water getting in the way. Personal preference, of course…and Becca Stevens was his.

"I brought towels," she said, spluttering again and then visibly shivering. Goosebumps erupted all down her arms.

Jack pushed to his feet and crossed over to sweep up the towels she'd left at the foot of the bush he had seen her hide behind earlier. When he turned to join her again, something struck him as strange. As…missing. Becca was sitting straighter, alert. With a curious gaze, she scanned the water.

Jack's throat thickened.

Where the hell was the dog?

Nine

"Can you see him anywhere?" Becca asked.

When Jack handed over a towel but didn't reply, she called Chichi's name nice and loud. Only eerie silence, sprinkled with cicada clicks, came back. She called again, and as the seconds ticked by, a feeling of dread filled her.

"He must be around somewhere," Jack said, lashing a towel around his hips before helping Becca to her feet as she wrapped her towel under her arms.

"I haven't seen him since I dived in," she said, scanning the woods for any sign.

Holding the towel around her chest, she crossed to the water's edge and called again. A sick feeling built high in her stomach and rose in her throat. When Jack, being supportive, gripped her shoulder, emotion prickled behind her nose.

Keep it together. Don't panic. Not yet.

Becca had lived alongside people, including babies and young children, who'd been forced to survive without adequate or clean water, with barely enough to eat, and little or no prospect of bettering their lives in a way most folks here took for granted. During her Peace Corps days, she'd kept strong, kept going. Rarely had she shed a tear, not because she hadn't felt anguish and despair, but because time spent crying was less time being productive. Being a positive role model.

And yet here she was, tears in her eyes, because she'd lost sight of a little dog.

But there was more to it than that. She'd been so self-absorbed in satisfying those urges, she hadn't given another thought to Hailey's dog. To her friend's four-legged baby. How would she explain that?

"Has he been here before?" Jack asked.

"Not to the lake, but he loves splashing around in the surf and diving into Hailey's pool at home. He likes the water."

"Yeah. I got that. He's probably dog-paddling up a storm right now, swimming across from the other side."

Becca crossed her arms, hugging herself, as she scanned the area again. Everything was so still. She called out his name, and then called it again, more loudly. As loudly as she could.

Jack gently turned her to face him. Holding her gaze with his, he gave a brave smile. "I'll find him, okay? You have my word."

His promise was supposed to make her feel better. But what was Jack's word really worth? He wasn't renowned for jumping on a steed and galloping to anyone's rescue. Angelica might disagree, but she was clinging to any port in the storm her father's death and will had brewed up.

"If we can't find him—" she said.

"We'll find him."

"But if we can't...how will I ever tell Hailey? She loves that dog like a child."

Jack skirted around in front of Becca and herded her back toward the trees, away from the lake. "You sit. I'll search. Deal?"

She didn't argue, but she had no intention of sitting back and doing nothing.

They quickly changed back into their clothes and Jack set off to circumnavigate the lake. Every now and then he brought cupped hands to his mouth and called out Chichi's name. As Becca headed off the other way, she sent up a prayer.

When she told Hailey this story, she needed it to have a happy ending.

It didn't look good.

Jack was halfway around the lake, calling out the pooch's name, searching the scrub nearest the water's edge. Not a peep. He'd assumed that Chichi had been paddling by himself in the lake before this.

Now he felt worse than any names reporters or broken businessmen had ever called him. Why hadn't he even given the little guy, who'd been paddling furiously, a second thought? Obviously because he had other things on his mind.

It was getting dark and he'd scoured most of the perimeter of the lake when he decided to head back. Becca had set off in the opposite direction. Looking back now and then, he'd seen her either wandering into or coming out of the woods, searching among the trees and shrubs. They'd both been calling for over an hour.

When they met back at the pier, Jack wrapped Becca in his arms. After a moment, she hugged him back. He grazed his lips through her hair. "We'd better go while there's still some light."

She nodded against his chest and then they walked hand in hand back down the trail. It might as well have been a funeral march. He couldn't help this situation, but he could at least try to keep Becca's mind on other things.

"We never had a cabin in the woods growing up," he said, giving her hand a squeeze.

"Don't suppose you need one when you own a five-star chalet in the snow."

She wasn't serious but there wasn't a hint of a tease in her voice, either. He tried again.

"What were the other kids in your family like?"

"I was the youngest, then Emily, Abigail and Faith."

"Still keep in touch?"

"Emily's in the U.K. now. She married a doctor."

"Good for her."

"Abigail is an elementary school teacher and Faith is travelling the world. She's in Burma at the moment, I think."

"Did you share any time with them here at the lake house?"

"Not recently. I've had Hailey up a couple of times."

She lowered her head and he tried to pick up their pace, to distract her from thinking about the dog and because night was falling fast. They needed to get back to the cabin.

"Anyone else?" he asked.

"A couple of friends from the office."

"Any male friends?"

She gave him a look. "You really want to know?"

He shrugged. *Your call.*

She didn't exactly grin. "Although it's rather personal… no. I've never brought any male friends to the cabin."

"You don't want to get personal?"

"I don't have anything to hide. What you see is what you get."

"What I see is a beautiful, feisty, determined woman who always puts others before herself."

Instead of a smile, the compliment brought on a frown. "Don't overdo it."

He blew out a breath. Guess it was going to be a long, cold night. So he might as well say what he felt.

"Has anyone ever told you that you have trouble accepting compliments?"

"I don't need compliments."

"Because you're tough."

"Because I already feel fine with who I am."

"Whereas I need lots of work."

She only looked the other way. Her hand felt limp in his. He had the sense she might be more comfortable severing the link. On one level, that annoyed him. Not an hour ago, she'd come apart in his arms as if it was her last feel-good moment before the world ended. He'd thought they'd been pretty tight then.

On the other hand, he understood…she felt gutted. He felt like crap, too.

By the time they made it back to the cabin, Becca wished she'd never heard the name Jack Reed. But not for the reasons he might have thought. She didn't blame Jack one bit for Chichi's disappearance. That dog had been her responsibility and she'd screwed up.

During the search, she'd not only thought ahead to Hailey's tears when she discovered the news, but also sifted through every grain of logic that said it was a good idea to kidnap Jack for a few days. She'd believed that coming here—experiencing this with her—would touch and bring out his more humble, benevolent side.

But Jack had been in the game a long time. Did she have any hope of swaying his plans to take over Lassiter Media and do what instinct told him to do: make a huge profit off selling the company piecemeal? No one could convince Angelica of Jack's deeper motives, just as no one could have told Becca she should have kept from sticking her nose in.

But not everything could be fixed, including, it would seem, her physical attraction toward Jack. Today she'd let her emotions rule her head in a spectacular way. On one level she didn't regret the time they'd spent in the lake together. She had never imagined that such intensity of sensation could truly exist. The height of her climax had turned her inside out.

On another far more practical level, while she had not set out to use the possibility of sex as a motivator, the fact remained that Jack had agreed to this challenge not because he thought for a moment she might be able to change his mind in a week about taking over Lassiter Media, but because a woman had confronted and intrigued him. Getting closer to her had been a challenge in itself. She'd pretty much handed herself to him on a platter. She was no different, in that regard, from any other woman he'd successfully seduced.

So why did she feel as if what had happened between them in the lake had been special? Why did she feel as if it truly mattered to him? Maybe because it had mattered to her. She felt a connection with Jack that made her want to leave their other, more complicated worlds behind.

When they got to the cabin, the door was ajar. In her stupid hurry to catch up with Jack, she'd bolted without shutting the damn thing. Now she walked in first.

"Want me to light a fire?" he asked, following her inside.

"It's not cold enough."

"Might get cold later."

He was trying to be supportive. He truly felt bad about how this afternoon had ended. He'd done his best to try to find poor Chichi.

Turning to him, she found a smile. "Thanks for trying to find him. I appreciate it."

In the shadows, she couldn't make out his face other than by the moonlight slanting in through the doorway.

"Becca…I'm sorry. I don't know what else to say."

"You don't need to say anything. Just sit with me awhile. Who knows? He might still come back." Chichi might not have drowned or been bitten by a snake or—

Becca caught a tear as it ran down her cheek. She apologized. "I'm not usually such a baby."

"You're not being a baby. You have feelings. Everyone has feelings."

"Even you."

"Yeah." She imagined she saw his smile. "Even me."

She reached up on tiptoe, rested a palm on his shirt and dotted a kiss on his cheek. "I'll get the lantern."

"You sit down," he said. "I don't need you tripping over something and breaking your leg."

"But I know this place—"

"And I'm telling you…*asking* you…please. Let me."

She surrendered and felt her way around to sit on the couch in front of the unlit fireplace. A moment later, a bright light from the main bedroom illuminated a wedge of the wooden floor in front of her. Telling herself that they would find Chichi tomorrow, and all would be well, she waited for Jack to return. Instead he called out.

"Becca, can you come here?"

She pushed to her feet and followed the light. Jack stood next to the set of drawers. He held the lantern high so most of the room was lit. Looking at the partly made bed, he grinned as he said, "Look who the cat dragged in."

Near the headboard, Becca saw two glowing eyes pop up. She blinked. And then she covered her mouth to smother the yelp—of delight, not fright.

Jack chuckled. "Seems Chichi decided to beat us home."

She rushed over, folded the cool little dog in her lap and smothered him in kisses. Wagging his tail, he lapped it all up.

"I know what this means," Jack said, moving closer.

Becca was still cuddling Chichi close. "What's that?"

"There won't be just the two of us sharing that bed tonight."

As low as she had felt a moment ago, now she felt as if she could fly. She didn't want to think about any regrets she might have in the morning. As Chichi jumped off the bed and leapt onto the camper cot, she only wanted to celebrate.

Ten

Becca reached up and pulled him down. As her mouth latched onto his, they fell back onto the bed.

Sometime later, when she let him come up for air, Jack arched a brow.

"Does this mean we have to get naked?"

They were lying facing each other. Now she sat up, grabbed the hem of his shirt and pulled it up. Then she dropped warm, hungry kisses all over his chest while her fingers kneaded his sides.

Her mouth slid lower and lower. The tip of her tongue was circling his navel when she unzipped his fly. Jack pushed up on his elbows. If she was about to do what he thought she would do, he was all for it. He helped her pull off his pants and boxer briefs. Then she snatched the dress off over her head. The bra landed on the coat stand in the corner. He wasn't sure where the panties went.

He was sitting at the foot of the bed while she stood before him. Ready to go, he fell back and then shot up again.

"Condoms," he said, ready to spring over to his bag for supplies.

But Becca was slotting herself between his parted thighs. Her breasts were at eye level. What was a man to do?

He dropped slow, moist kisses around one nipple while plucking and lightly pinching the other. Her fingers drove through his hair, over the back of his scalp then across to each shoulder as she arched into him and made noises in her throat that only excited him more.

His other hand fanned down the curve of her ribs, waist, hip. When his fingers slid between her legs and found her wet, he remembered why he'd sat up in the first place.

While he sucked and plucked and gently rubbed, he spoke around that nipple. "Rubbers…"

She pulled his head away, snatched a penetrating kiss that blew his mind and then lowered onto her knees on the floor. A second before her lips met the tip of his erection, he heard her murmur, "Not yet."

As her head lowered more, a series of bone-melting sensations rippled over his skin. At first she simply held him in her mouth. Then her tongue got into the act, swirling around the ridge, rolling one way then the other, tickling the tip. When she began to hum, the vibration at the base of her throat drifted along her tongue and teeth.

He clutched the sheet and clenched his jaw.

He wasn't normally this excited this soon. It had to be all the buildup—in the lake, coming home—and because she knew just what to do and how to do it, as if they had been together like this before. Of course, before this week, she would have jumped off a cliff rather than…well, do what she was doing now.

He shifted enough to scoop her around the waist and lift her up and onto the bed. As she lay there looking at him with hungry eyes, he cautioned her with a finger.

"Stay right there. Don't move."

With a cheeky grin, she crossed her heart.

He found his bag, ripped the condom box open and, crossing back, rolled the rubber on. Becca's arms were tucked under the pillow behind her head. Her hair had dried. In the lantern light, the mussed waves glistened around her face. Then she drew up one knee, angled her hips in a provocative pose, and he crawled up the mattress until he was kissing her again. He couldn't bring her close enough as they rolled together on the sheets.

His breathing was heavy by the time he urged her over onto her back and positioned himself between her thighs. As he entered her slowly, he watched her eyes widen, her back arch and lips part. Then she smiled. He wanted to say how beautiful she was, not just her face or her body, but the way she made him feel—truly alive for the first time in years.

When her legs wrapped around his thighs and her pelvis slanted up, he closed his eyes and gave himself over to sensation.

He'd wanted this, their first time together, to last all night. She fit him so well—everywhere. The physical friction building between them was the sweetest he'd ever known. And as heat began to blaze and then to rage, Jack found himself picturing them here together like this for more than two nights.

For longer than either one could ever allow.

Becca's entire body was left buzzing—floating. All the rumors were true. Jack Reed was not only smoking hot in bed, in her opinion, he was legendary.

They were lying on their backs side by side, both gazing blindly at the ceiling. Basking in the afterglow, they were still panting and smiling. Becca's skin was cooling. The payoff had been so unbelievably good, she only wanted to do it again.

"I wonder if that dog planned this," he said.

"What do you mean?"

"If Chichi hadn't wandered off," he explained, "we wouldn't be here doing this."

"If we hadn't lost him in the first place," she pointed out, "we would have done this beside the lake."

"And right now mosquitoes would be feasting on our backsides." He kissed her nose. "Our little friend did us a favor."

"After half scaring me death."

"He didn't know."

She laughed. "Jack Reed, crusader for misunderstood mutts."

"Make that misunderstood *ugly* mutts."

"Not kind, and yet I can see it on a T-shirt. On the letter-head of a charity. Maybe you should get one of your own."

"A dog?"

"And a charity."

He shifted up on an elbow and cupped his jaw in his palm. "Maybe I should."

His smile was so close, and with his heavy hand resting on the dip of her waist... Becca felt so lucky. And somehow also sad. If she didn't know Jack's background, if he wasn't so forthright in embracing his less-flattering side, she might be fooled into believing they were made for each other.

In reality, of course, two people couldn't be less suited to each other. This physical chemistry might be explosive, but what a person believed in was a thousand times more important than how skilled and connected they were in the bedroom. She stood for sacrifice and the betterment of society. Jack stood for self-gain, for power at the expense of anything and anyone who stood in his way.

"Does the lake have fish?" he asked, toying with a wave of her hair.

"My dad used to fish here all the time."

"Any poles around?"

"In the shed." She drew a wiggling line down the middle of his steamy chest. "You like fishing?"

"My father took me fly-fishing a couple of times."

"Fond memories?"

"Sure. We didn't get to spend that much time together."

"Why's that?"

"He ran his own company. That means putting in the extra hours when employees get to go home to their families."

"If it was his company, he could have made a choice to go home rather than stay."

"Not that simple. Before I came along, my father was bankrupt. They lost their house and more than a few fair-weather friends. At the same time my mother landed in the hospital with pneumonia. She almost died. On one of those fishing trips, Dad told me that when he thought she might not pull through, he'd made a vow. If only she lived, if they could spend a long and happy life together, he would take care of her the way she deserved."

"He blamed himself for her illness?"

"He felt responsible for his family. She recovered and their luck seemed to change. He started up another company, finance lending this time, and it took off. But he always had one eye on the past, the other on the future. He never allowed himself to drop the ball. His priority was making sure we were cared for."

"Even if he couldn't share what was most precious of all."

"His time? I knew he loved us both. But there were sacrifices. You can't have everything."

"Do you see much of them now?"

"They passed away ten years ago within months of each other."

"That must have been hard."

"We've all got to go sometime. Better to go in your seventies than…" His jaw tensed and he looked away.

Was he remembering the woman he had loved in college? Did he wonder what they might have shared and conquered together if she had lived? Becca wasn't sure he would have taken his father's route and dedicated his life to a company in order to ensure security for his family. She would rather believe that he'd have taken his own son fly-fishing often—spent quality time with those he loved.

Jack sat up. "Hey, you want a beer? A glass of wine?"

"Beer," she said, reaching over the side of the bed to find her dress.

"Stay put. I'll find the bathroom, clean up and bring back supplies. Can I take the light?"

"Be my guest."

While he was gone and she was left in the shadows, Becca shimmied under the top sheet and waited. She heard Chichi's collar rattle from the cot in the corner as he scratched himself. She'd had plans to set Jack to work while they were here. Chopping wood, fixing loose shingles, sanding back walls, cooking simple meals. Nothing so out of the ordinary for normal folk. Her goal had been to highlight the difference between the big-time "haves" and people who had to struggle. There were plenty of them out there.

There wasn't much work going on at the moment.

Soon, he was back carrying the ice chest in one hand, flashlight in the other. Becca took the light and he jumped in under the sheet and then set the chest down between them. As he cracked open one beer and handed it over, she picked up the thread of their conversation.

"Sounds as if you had good parents."

"I was lucky," he admitted, cracking open one for himself. They saluted each other and pulled down a mouthful. Becca didn't drink beer often, but in this setting, on this night, it felt right.

"I've never found out who my birth mother was," she said, resting the beer on her lap. "I didn't want to complicate anyone's life by dropping back in."

"Isn't it usually the other way around? A biological parent not wanting to make waves in the adult child's life?"

"I figure it might not be easy, but there are ways to track down a baby who's been gobbled up in the system. If she didn't want to know, it's better left alone."

"You never wanted to know the reasons?"

"Not anymore. Can't change yesterdays. And I didn't have such a hard time, even those first eleven years."

"Were you with lots of families?"

"Two others. I was provided for. Nobody abused me. But…" She brought the beer to her lips, swallowed another mouthful and confessed what she hadn't told anyone before. "I knew something was missing. Something key. Sometimes I felt…*invisible.*" Sometimes she felt that way still. But not with Jack. Even right from the start. "It's hard to describe."

"Did you feel that way a lot?"

"Whenever I did, I read. Sometimes the same book over and over."

"What was your favorite?"

"When I was very young, *Cinderella.*"

"A classic. Like the Bambino."

She smiled. "I fell in love with the idea of a fairy godmother. When all the lights went out at night, I'd sit up in bed and gaze out the window for what seemed like hours. I thought if only I wished hard enough, all my dreams would come true."

"What dreams?"

"I was an overweight, painfully shy girl. I wouldn't say boo to save myself. But in my dreams I was a princess, like Cinders. I simply needed my godmother to wave her wand and work her magic."

He was grinning. "Well, of course."

"If ever I saw a mouse," she went on, "I would close my eyes and wish for it to change into a beautiful white steed. I'd daydream that my dress was a gorgeous billowing gown made of white satin. Naturally a prince would happen along, fall on one knee and beg me to marry him."

Jack's eyes were smiling. "Naturally."

"The ring he'd ask me to wear was either a big diamond circled by priceless rubies, or a pearl surrounded by a sparkling sea of sapphires. Something right out of yesteryear."

"And then?"

Becca put her beer down. "Then I grew up, got a degree, joined the Peace Corps."

His expression changed. "Tell me about that."

"I served as a volunteer in the Dominican Republic for two years."

"That would be right after college?"

"Uh-huh. I helped to teach the youth how to make good choices. We talked to women about reproduction health and nutrition. There's so much poverty and unemployment. It's hard to imagine my life back there now. Those two years shaped me more than anything before or since. I know the true value of a safe, soft place to land."

"I had dreams of saving the world, too, once."

"*No.* Really?"

"I'd finished my engineering business degree. I was going to fly to Africa to help build housing."

Was he serious? "Jack, have you ever told anyone else that?"

"What? And destroy my image?"

She grinned. "So, you were going by yourself?"

"With my girlfriend. My fiancée. We were going to leave everything behind. Start fresh."

Lying on her side, Becca laid her cheek on her outstretched arm and searched his eyes.

"What was she like?"

He seemed to think back. "Krystal was soft. Delicate. She was studying criminal law. Her father was a defense attorney, and then became a judge later in his career. I never thought she was cut out for it. She didn't fit with the idea of courtroom drama and getting murderers off on a technicality. She was gentle. Easily hurt. Entirely giving."

Becca's heart was beating faster.

"You wanted to protect her."

Like Jack's father had wanted to protect his mom.

"I imagined us married with a couple of boys," he said. "I'd come home from work every day and she'd have a delicious dinner waiting. Later, while she took some downtime, I'd play with the kids."

Becca smiled softly. "I can imagine you doing that." She really could. "Can I ask…how did she die?"

His jaw tightened. "Her father was one mean son of a gun. Krystal was never good enough for the judge. She was an only child, so it was up to her to follow in her dad's giant footsteps. Carry on the legacy. She began to flunk classes. She wasn't looking after herself. When she came down with mono, it laid her up for weeks. Then we spent Thanksgiving at her parents'. Big mistake. Her father went from cool, to frosty, to flat-out belligerent. At the table, he started attacking her, telling her that she had to try harder. If that was her best, it wasn't near good enough."

Becca felt ill. "Poor girl."

"I gave him a piece of my mind. Then I was in *everyone's* bad books."

It was true. A person could say what they like about

their own family, but God help anyone else who tried to bring them down.

"Krystal was depressed for weeks after that. Then, a few days before Christmas, the dark cloud seemed to lift. She was smiling again. She said that she'd come to accept that she couldn't get away from disappointing her father, but that was okay."

Becca knew what was coming.

A muscle in his jaw flexed before Jack ended, "She didn't see that Christmas morning. I found her in the bathroom."

"Oh, Jack ..."

"Her father blamed me. Hell, *I* blamed me."

Was this the reason he'd looked so distant when they'd visited that school—the day she'd lectured him about vulnerable young adults? He had already learned that lesson on his own.

"You shouldn't blame yourself," she said, holding his hand. "She needed professional help."

"Instead her boyfriend added to the pressure." He exhaled. "So, you see, sometimes it's not so good to be handed your future, whether you think you want it or not. Big shoes are hard to fill."

Was that his way of justifying his position with Angelica? If they should succeed in overthrowing Evan McCain, was that perspective meant to stave off guilt over persuading Angelica to later sell off the pieces?

He studied her face for a long moment before casting a look at the ice chest. Shifting his hand from under hers, he flipped open the lid again and put a casual note in his voice.

"So, what else have we got? Eggs, bacon, tomatoes? You have gas in the kitchen?"

"Yeah. I do."

Becca was still processing everything he'd divulged.

How many more layers were there to this man? What other wounds was he covering up? Her first eleven years of her life hadn't been a picnic, but she hadn't had anyone close to her die. Jack had lost the woman he had loved as well as both his parents. Some people grieved by putting up a wall. Shutting off certain parts of themselves. Was that Jack?

"What say I whip you up an omelet?" he said.

She tried to be light. "You cook?"

"Not well."

"Can you chop wood?"

"If required."

It wasn't cool enough for a fire. Becca peered inside the ice chest. "There's crackers and strawberries and three kinds of cheese. And look at this…" She drew out a package. "Belgian chocolate."

"Even better than Danishes."

She broke off two pieces and slotted one bit in his mouth, the other in her own.

"I should mention that I have a chocolate addiction," she said around her mouthful.

"Chocolate's good for you."

He popped another square into her mouth and she smiled as she took in every line of his face.

"If you're a chocoholic," he said, "you need to try this."

He broke off another piece of chocolate and set a strawberry on top. "Open up," he said, and she did.

As she chewed and sighed, he made his own chocolate-strawberry stack.

"Oh, God." She sighed. "This is so good."

His lips came close to taste hers. "I totally agree."

Eleven

After their picnic and talk in bed, Becca fell asleep in Jack's arms.

He lay there for he didn't know how long, thinking back on how he'd opened up about that piece of his past. The words had come remarkably easy. The emotion hadn't been as painful as he'd remembered. Time healed all wounds? Maybe that was true. It was the scars he couldn't seem to kick.

Jack closed his eyes for a moment. When he opened them again, morning light was streaking in through the window, warming the room with a gauzy golden glow. Smiling, Jack stretched. *Man,* he felt good. And the reason was lying right here alongside of him.

He reached out to bring Becca close—and came up empty. The only sign of her was the impression left on the sheet.

Jack sat up.

The cot was empty, too. Other than birds chirping and

squawking outside, all was quiet. The screened window was open, letting in pine-scented fresh air. No smog. No traffic. No meetings.

No phone calls?

Was there even reception out here?

Jack swung out of bed, grabbed some jeans and pulled them on. Then he found his phone. Some texts and three voicemails. One from Logan, one from Angelica and one from David Baldwin.

Wearing cutoffs and a T-shirt that read "Choose Happiness," Becca entered the room. Her flawless face broke into a big smile. "You're up!"

Something pleasant tugged in Jack's gut. He crossed over, folded her up in his arms and nuzzled the top of her head. She felt soft and warm and smelled like sunshine. If Angelica was okay when he called back, maybe they could stay an additional couple of days. Or three, or four.

"I missed you," he murmured against her hair.

She laughed. "You've been awake two minutes."

"One minute."

Pulling away, she spotted the phone in his hand. When her smile cooled, he felt a spike of guilt—which he shouldn't.

"I wasn't sure if we got reception out this far," he said.

"It's patchy. Any messages?"

"A few."

While her eyes still shone, her mouth tightened. "Anything important?"

"You don't want to know."

"Angelica?" Jack nodded. "You going to call her back?" She held up her hands. "Sorry. Stupid question. She might be planning a coup for this afternoon. You wouldn't want to miss that."

Jack caught her as she turned to leave. "Becca, this was always a tricky situation."

She kept her gaze on the wooden floor. "I didn't think it'd get *this* tricky."

Ah, hell.

He brought her close again and, lifting her chin, searched those sparkling green eyes. "Are you sorry we came?"

"Up until a second ago, for so many reasons, I wasn't. I wanted to take you away from everything that drives your need to win. I wanted you to live a simple life and appreciate it, even for a couple of days. I thought you might see how little people need, and how easy it would be for everyone to have that if we all cared enough. But now…"

"What we shared last night was amazing. But I still have to help Angelica. I just *have* to."

"Because someone has a gun to your head?"

Jack struggled and then admitted, "I can't explain."

"No need. It's pretty obvious."

He studied her wounded, defiant look and then put the phone down on the side table.

Her gaze snapped from the phone back to him. "You're not going to call her?"

"Angelica can wait."

But then his phone rang. Becca swept it up and held it out for him, daring him to refuse, hoping that he would. He wanted to ignore the call, but now it had rung a bigger part wanted to reconnect and plug into what was going on beyond the walls of this cabin. He couldn't walk away from this deal, not even for Becca.

He took the phone, connected. It wasn't Angelica.

"Hope I didn't catch you too early," David Baldwin said. "I left a message—"

Annoyed, Jack cut in. "What can I do for you?"

"I'm having a get-together this afternoon. I know you're probably busy."

Chichi pranced in with a stick between his small, pointy teeth. Jack turned toward the window view. "A bit, yeah."

"But if you could make it over, just for a few moments… it's important."

"David, I really don't think—"

"Don't give me your answer now." He gave a time for the event. "At the shop. Hope to see you there."

David Baldwin could hope all he liked.

Chichi was going to town, chewing his stick on the cot. Becca, however, had disappeared.

As Jack headed for the doorway, she marched by, carrying the ice chest. He strode out and took it from her. *For Pete's sake.*

"What exactly is the rush?" he asked.

"It's time to go."

"You said two days and two nights."

"I've changed my mind. Things have gotten off track. This won't work."

Jack put down the chest and turned off his phone. "Weren't we fixing bacon and eggs?" Amid the giggling and kissing last night, there'd been some mention of cooking breakfast before she'd fallen asleep.

"I'd rather just get back on the road. You know…get back to reality."

"I didn't mean to upset you."

She knotted her arms over her chest. "I'm not upset with you. I'm upset with *me*. For a second there, I'd actually talked myself into believing that I might have reached your human side. A *caring* side that didn't have stealing and then raping Lassiter Media as next on his to-do list. But you can't wait to get back into it."

Jack flinched. Well, that stung.

"One day," he said, "I promise, we'll sit down and I'll give you the lowdown on this Lassiter business from my perspective. Just…not today. I can't today." He filed his fingers back through her silky hair and waited for her to meet his gaze. "Now, can I make us a coffee?"

"That won't fix anything."

"It sure won't hurt."

When he grinned, she bit her lip, exhaled and finally nodded. As they headed back to the kitchen, she said, "I guess there's still a part of me who believes in a fairy godmother. She was just here, expecting a miracle."

"Could be that's what I like most about you," he said. "Your faith." He stopped and turned her in the circle of one arm.

"You mean my temper," she said.

"Your tenacity."

"My stubborn streak."

"I like this about you, too."

His lips met hers and lingered there. Closing his eyes, he drank in all that sassy, strong-headed goodness. When he drew away, her eyes narrowed even as those succulent lips twitched.

"Next you'll be suggesting we take our coffee back to bed."

"Well, just remember." He lowered his head to kiss her properly. "It was your idea."

When she brought it up again, Jack didn't try to talk her out of leaving the cabin. She didn't need for matters between the two of them to get any more complicated than they already were, and he obviously needed to get back to see what Angelica was up to.

He'd tried to phone Angelica a number of times. When he'd failed to reach her, he'd grown more and more preoccupied. He even admitted that he wondered if Angelica was purposely avoiding his calls now because she planned to do something he would stop if he could. When they finally got on the road after lunch, Becca couldn't shake the sense of guilt.

She had allowed her emotions to get the better of her where Jack was concerned. She'd taken him to the cabin not to give in to the attraction brewing between them, but to somehow help him gain perspective away from his cut-throat corporate world. She wanted to show him in a hands-on way he would remember that lots of people went without even the bare necessities. Had her scheme done any good at all, or had she only made matters worse?

Still, what Jack and she had shared at the cabin was more than physical. At least it had been for her. However much she abhorred Jack's business tactics and egocentric mind-set, whenever they had been together in an intimate sense, she hadn't been able to help falling just a little in love with him.

Chichi had sat on Becca's lap all the drive back to Santa Monica. When Jack pulled into the quiet beachside parking lot in a space right next to Hailey's café, the dog was quivering with excitement. Then Becca opened the car door; she couldn't stop Chichi from bolting up the ramp into the café's rear entrance.

Jack got out and hauled the ice chest off the backseat.

"Want to chow down while we're here?" Becca asked, joining him.

"Best to keep going."

He was eager to get back to L.A. He needed to call on Angelica, keep that Lassiter takeover ball rolling and on track. Becca had felt his preoccupation building for the whole drive back. Now, as they walked up the café's ramp together, he seemed disconnected.

As they made their way around the veranda, Hailey and Chichi appeared.

"How was the trip?" Hailey asked. "Hope Chichi behaved himself."

Jack set down the chest. As they took their usual seats and Hailey poured coffee, Becca let her friend know what had happened with Chichi the previous day at the lake… minus the bits about Jack and her being, well, otherwise occupied.

"I'm sorry," Becca said. "We should have kept a closer eye on him."

Hailey waved it off. "Way I see it, he probably just wanted to give you two some space."

When she flicked a knowing glance Jack's way, he held his expression, no hint of cheekiness or denial. But Becca's chest tightened. In his mind, he'd already moved on. What they had shared at the lake was in the past. He was back in corporate-raider mode and focused on bringing down his current target.

When neither Jack nor Becca commented, Hailey's expression grew concerned. "Oh, God," she murmured. "You don't know. There's no TV out at the cabin."

Jack's brow creased as he sat forward. "What happened?"

"It was on this morning," Hailey went on.

"You mean the interview from the reporter who ambushed us yesterday?" Becca asked.

"There were clips from that interview…." Hailey pressed her lips together. "It's the photos that got everyone talking."

Becca suddenly felt dizzy and she couldn't feel her face.

"What photos?" she groaned. She wasn't sure she wanted to know.

"You must have been followed," Hailey said. "They had shots of you both in that lake, taken with a telescopic lens, so they were kinda grainy. But it's pretty clear what you all were doing."

While Jack sat back like he'd been shot in the chest, the

knot of horror in Becca's stomach pulled apart and spread through every inch of her body. Everything around her, other than Jack's scowl, seemed to funnel back and fade to black.

Becca was always fighting the hard fight, standing up for morals and justice. Now she shut her eyes as that darkness enveloped her.

Despite keeping an eye out, Hailey said they must have been followed. Had they been followed back here, too?

She had to phone the office again and make certain Evans McCain understood. Things had gotten—confused, but she was still one hundred percent on his side.

"There's more," Hailey said, wincing.

Jack rubbed his brow. "Of course there is."

"Angelica Lassiter has called a press conference," Hailey went on, "scheduled for this afternoon."

Jack thumped the table and everyone, including Chichi, jumped. When he pushed to his feet, the action sent his chair skating and clattering into the one behind it.

Becca stood, too, hugged her friend and whispered in her ear, "I'll call you later."

Becca followed Jack around the veranda and down the ramp. Before he reached the driver's-side door of her Bambino, he stopped abruptly and spun around. She almost ran into him.

He held out his hand. "Keys."

Becca fumbled in her bag and slapped them in his palm. "You're going to see Angelica," she said.

"As soon as humanly possible."

Jack threw open the car door. As Becca skirted around and jumped in the passenger side, he turned the key in the ignition. The lights flashed up on the dash…but the engine didn't kick over. He growled and tried again.

Nothing.

He set his teeth, raised his fists, but held off somehow from smashing down on the wheel. If Becca was upset, Jack was livid. And then...

Things went from bad to a hundred times worse.

Twelve

"That's just great. That's *exactly* what I need."

Becca scowled across at him. "You're not the only one stuck in this car, you know."

"It's your car!"

As the tabloid show truck sailed into the parking lot and pulled behind them blocking their escape, Becca opened her mouth then simply sat back and crossed her arms tightly over her T-shirt while Jack brought up an app on his phone and sent a text for a cab.

He'd apologize for raising his voice later. Right now he needed to get them the hell out of this predicament. He didn't care who had tipped them off again or whether he and Becca had been followed the entire time. The director of the Lassiter Foundation had been seen repeatedly with the man who wanted to bring the whole lot down. He needed to get Becca out of this mess then he'd find Angelica before she purged in front of a microphone and said something they both might regret at that press conference.

When Angelica had wavered the other day, Jack thought he had been persuasive enough to get her back to where he needed her to be. Once again she had seemed set upon a path that would lead to a takeover of the company that was rightfully hers. But when she'd called this morning early and he hadn't been able to get in contact with her since, Jack had begun to worry. If Becca hadn't decided to call her cabin stay short, he'd have insisted.

As the camera crew and the reporter from the other day loped over, he threw open the door. "Get out of the car," he told Becca.

He met her around her side, grabbed her hand and headed for the road. She had to trot to keep up.

"Where are we going?"

"We're getting the hell out of Dodge."

As they reached the pavement, she yanked her hand from his. Her face was flushed but her bearing was almost regal.

"I'm not going," she said. "You've had Angelica dancing on your strings. Everyone knows she doesn't do anything without consulting you first. If Angelica's called a press conference without your permission or advice, it can only mean she's distancing herself from you. It might even mean that she's decided to step down from a takeover bid. I'm not going to tag along while you try to badger her into changing her mind."

The cab he'd ordered swerved into the gutter. Swinging open the door, he eyeballed Becca. "You coming?"

"I'll hold my head up and face the firing squad square on, thank you."

He had to admire her courage. "When you have a moment," he said, "I'll give you a lesson on how to avoid unnecessary trouble."

"You haven't done such a great job of it lately."

So it would seem. He should have flat-out refused

to give Becca an audience in the first place. Of course that would've meant missing out on getting to know her more—a once-in-a-lifetime experience. There'd never be another Becca.

"I'll call," he told her.

"Please don't."

"I can't change your mind?"

She only crossed her arms. Defiant to the end.

Jack hung his head, considered the repercussions and, leaving the cab door open, joined her again. "Then I'll stay, too."

Her eyes widened as her arms dropped to her sides. "I don't need you."

"Right now I think we need each other."

Stopping in position before them, the reporter shot out her first question.

"Mr. Reed," she began, "what do you have to say about the photos of yourself and Ms. Stevens circulating this morning?"

Jack surprised Becca. He didn't growl. Didn't try to divert the issue. He simply looped his arm around her waist, tugged her closer and announced, "Ms. Stevens and I are late for an engagement. So, if you'll excuse us…"

Then he crowded Becca toward the open cab door, leaving her no chance to argue. He scooted in the backseat after her. As he reached to close the door, the reporter persisted.

"Mr. Reed, wait…did you say engagement? You and Becca Stevens are engaged to be married? Does Angelica Lassiter know? Are you backing out of a takeover bid of Lassiter Media?"

The door slammed shut. The reporter's microphone hit the glass. Tires squealed as the cab pulled out.

"Where to?" the driver asked in an Eastern European accent.

"Beverly Hills."

Looking in the rearview mirror, the cabbie reached for a candy dispenser on the dash. He shook a mint into his mouth and sucked for a moment. "You are Jack Reed and the lady from the Lassiter charity, yes? I see pictures of you on TV."

Becca wanted to smack her forehead. Seemed everyone had seen those photos except them.

"No worries, Mr. Reed," the cabbie said with a lopsided grin. "I will lose those leeches. My mother-in-law, she worked for a big-time newspaper. She's still Mrs. Snoopidy Snoops." He sneered. "Always on my case, sticking in her nose where it might get cut off."

The cab swerved off the main drag down a side street.

"We get back on the highway a few miles down." The cabbie looked back at them over a shoulder. "Feel free to talk. What happens in cab, stays in cab."

After a few moments, Jack dared to look across at Becca. Her lips were tight, cheeks were pink. Her hands were balled up in fists at her sides.

"You tricked me," she growled.

"I did what I thought was right."

"You did what was right for *you*. I told you—" she pointed to Jack's brow "—you've got rocks in your head if you think I'm going with you to talk to Angelica. If you do, I'll tell her that she's being a fool. That she's destroying her family over the illusion of power. I'll ask her where the hell she put her priorities."

In this mood, Jack had no doubt that she would.

"I'll drop you off at your office," he said.

She slumped back and held her head. "They'll probably lynch me."

"Then I'll drop you home."

"That's not really addressing the problem, is it, Jack?"

He shut his eyes, his patience running thin now.

"I don't know what you expect me to do," he said. "If

you're waiting for a halo to magically appear above my head and a plea for forgiveness, don't hold your breath."

She stared at the ceiling, tears in her eyes. "I'm a fool. I was attracted to you and I let that ruin everything."

"Depends on how you look at it."

Her voice was thick, resigned. "There's only one way to look at it."

He didn't think so. "I want to see you again, Becca." And he didn't care who knew.

She froze, mouth half-open, eyes wide with shock. Then she shook herself and self-righteousness ruled again.

"You actually want to throw more fuel on this fire? Maybe you want to screw with my affections so much that I'll crumble and lead a munity of Lassiter management and employees against McCain?"

"That's crazy talk."

"Yeah, well, maybe I'm crazy."

"We're not going to get anywhere if—"

"That's it, Jack. We, you and I, are not going to get anywhere. Because this is over. O-V-E-R."

Angelica sent another text after Jack had dropped Becca home. She asked that he meet her at Lassiter Grill. He tried to ignore the ball of unease growing in the pit of his gut. The location was a sure sign. For her to suggest they meet there, she must have reconciled with her brother, Dylan, the one who'd been left controlling interest of the Lassiter Grill Group, including the restaurant here in L.A.

Jack would hear what she had to say. Then, if there was any doubt whatsoever about her caving in to the terms of J.D.'s will, he'd do his damnedest to talk her out of it.

When the cab dropped him off, Jack gave the driver a huge tip. As he walked into the restaurant, with its trademark rustic elegance, he spotted Angelica at a booth not far from the floor-to-ceiling stone fireplace. She sat staring into her coffee cup, looking like a jumper about to take that last step.

"Hello, Angelica," he said, sitting opposite her.

Angelica's head came up. Her expression was scathing. "What in the name of God were you thinking?"

Jack thatched his fingers on the table in front of him. "You're referring to Becca Stevens."

"The company, particularly the foundation, has been hit hard enough by this tug-of-war. Why in the name of everything sane would you go and sleep with that woman?"

"I didn't exactly plan it, Ange. Or not the way it turned out anyway."

She straightened in her seat. "I spoke with Logan. He was speechless."

And Jack was supposed to...what? Go to his room for time-out? "I am an adult. I don't need to ask permission."

"You sure as hell do when you're dragging my name down along with hers." She shook her head, incredulous. "I thought you said you weren't trying to get Becca on our side."

"I wasn't."

She blinked and frowned. "So, this was purely for sport?"

His teeth set so hard, his jaw ached. "I like Becca Stevens."

"Well, that's a shame because you just destroyed her."

It was bad, but not that bad. And Jack sure as hell didn't know why he was copping all the blame. "Becca's an adult, too. I didn't tie her down."

"She's no match for you." Angelica's anger turned into concern. "No one is."

Time to get back on topic. He took a breath and focused. "You wanted to see me."

"I want to... I mean, I'm pretty sure that I want to..."

"Walk away from your rightful inheritance?"

She raised her voice. "I want things back the way they were."

"We *can't* go back. We can only go forward. With commitment and justice on our side." He believed that to his bones.

Her head slowly tilted as she evaluated him through narrowed eyes. "You're saying the words, but somehow you don't sound as convinced."

That was news to him. But, granted… "It's been a long battle. When things are worth fighting for, it's never easy."

"Becca Stevens didn't get to you, did she? Here I am thinking you've used her, but I wonder—"

"If she had an effect on me?" Jack threw up his hands. "You know, in fact, *yes,* she did. She's a special lady with a big heart and too many other assets to count." He leaned forward. "But none of that changes what you and I are trying to achieve. *Will* achieve. Just think, Angelica. You won't have to live with the label of the snubbed daughter of J. D. Lassiter for much longer."

Her eyes glistened with moisture.

"You're not as strong as J.D.," Jack said. "You're stronger. And when you need a rest, like now, I'm here to stand guard on the battlements."

She blew out a shaky breath, then rested her elbow on the table and held her brow. "You don't know what it feels like to have to choose, Jack."

He might consider her fortunate. He was never given a choice.

When Logan had informed him of the part he was to play in this unfolding drama, Jack had wanted to refuse. But a friend was a friend; that didn't change once they died. And so he had agreed to comply with the special clause in J.D.'s will, which was meant solely for him and Angelica. Since that day he'd led her closer and closer toward a corporate showdown against Evan and anyone who stood behind him. The way Jack had looked at it, either outcome would be a victory.

Now…he only wished Becca Stevens didn't have to be part of the collateral damage.

Angelica called off the press conference, and Jack left her in a better state, although he didn't have a lot of faith in what the immediate future might bring. Angelica was an educated, capable woman. But he wondered how soon she would have crumpled and given in to the terms of the will if he hadn't been stirring her pot.

Jack ordered another cab, his intentions being to call in at the office—the first time ever wearing jeans, unlike Ms. Stevens. Not that he was in the mood to sit behind a desk. Truth be known, he felt like fishing…beside a quiet lake, simply to enjoy the atmosphere, the fresh air. The company.

As eventful as his time with Becca had been, he had an ice cube's chance in hell of rekindling those flames. Which got him thinking…just how long had it been since he'd been with a woman? The press played up his womanizing past. Jack's take? If a guy was single and able, damned if he'd want to sit at home singing to his cats. But he wasn't as ruthless in that department as the media made out. Of course it wasn't every day a man came across someone as intriguing as Becca.

She was in every way his match, including her annoying headstrong streak. And when they made love…she was wild and smart and incredibly generous. There were times when she exhausted him. She *always* inspired him.

And he sincerely doubted she'd ever want to see his hide again.

Jack was tossing around whether to tell the driver to ditch his earlier address and simply take him home when his cell phone beeped with a text. He prayed it wasn't

Angelica. Hoped against hope it might be Becca. It was neither.

David Baldwin. Again.

Still hope to see you this afternoon.
Best, Dave.

Jack felt bad for the man. He wished he could help the way David wanted him to. That was out of the question. But there was something more he could do. He had an afternoon to fill in anyway.

The cab dropped Jack off in front of the Baldwin Boats office and factory. The signage across the front of the main building was faded. The *o* in boats was gone completely. The yard was free of workers. He glanced at his watch. After quitting time for the factory.

As he neared the entrance, an odd, prickling feeling ran over his skin. He'd just take five minutes to tell Baldwin that not only was the deal still on the table, he would up the offer. Becca was right. How much money did one man need? And Dave had mentioned in one of the conversations that he had six kids. *Six.* What a scary thought. Four boys, two girls. What was it like growing up in a houseful of siblings? Noisy. Scary. Certainly never lonely.

When the receptionist spotted him strolling in through the automatic entry doors, she shot to her feet.

"Oh! Mr. Reed. Dave was expecting you. Well, he'd hoped…" She grinned like a kid who'd discovered every tree in the backyard had turned into a ball of cotton candy. "I'll go tell him you're here."

As she scurried off, Jack strolled around the reception area. Framed photographs hung on the walls, pictures of power catamarans, officials at boat launches. Quite a few of David, the earliest from perhaps twenty years ago. Before putting the contract together, he'd had a full background check compiled. David was only a little older than Jack, although he looked at least, ten years older. Stress could do that to a person. And while Jack lived with stress, it wasn't the kind where he had to scramble to find the next mortgage payment, or wonder when the utilities might be turned off. He didn't have to worry every week whether or not he could make the payroll. Jack knew that had been Dave's dilemma pretty much since the recession had hit and turned the economy on its head.

Dave ambled out from his office, a big smile plastered on his face. When he held out his hand, Jack took a hold and shook. There was a lot to be said about a man's handshake and Dave Baldwin's was firm without being cocky.

"Jack, glad you could make it," Dave said, ushering him down the corridor. He was a tall man. Almost as tall as Jack.

"Seems I'm too late for that get together," Jack said. Looked like everyone else had gone.

"Not too late at all."

They sat in tub chairs in Dave's office, a room that overlooked the factory yard. Outside Jack saw a couple of fixed cranes, several boat molds, numerous trailers, trolleys meant to shift upward of six tons. There was plenty of value in those assets. From previous conversations, Jack knew that Dave would never consider downsizing, which would mean putting people on unemployment. Men of Dave's ilk lived by two mottos: natural attrition only, and the captain must go down with the ship.

"Can I get you a coffee, Jack?"

"Got a beer?"

Dave brought two back from a bar fridge tucked under a counter covered with engineering plans. Jack cracked open the beer and downed a couple of much appreciated mouthfuls.

"Hmm. Cold," he said.

"I like it so cold that my lips turn numb."

Jack grinned. "Me, too."

"Cheryl and I have four boys, you know?"

"You mentioned."

"Oldest turning twenty-one next spring. Old enough to drink, to vote. It's scary how quickly time goes. I was twenty-one when I first got into this business. I worked my rear end off. When the owner decided to retire, he asked if I wanted to buy in. I learned everything from that man. He was like a father to me."

"That's a long time in one place. I understand why you think of your employees as family."

"Family..." Studying the floor near his feet, David nodded deeply. "It's the most powerful word in the dictionary, don't you think? Just the idea of family makes a person feel warm and included." He caught Jack's gaze. "And sometimes a little overwhelmed."

Dave was looking at him so curiously, as if his face was a mask he wanted peeled back to see what lay underneath. Jack, however, couldn't help thinking about the Lassiter family, how it had all come together only to be recently torn apart.

"You have two daughters, too," Jack said.

"They're the youngest. Twins. Only six. My wife worries that we're old parents. That we might not be around to see our youngest grandkids. I tell her that our memory and our love will live on. Those girls, the boys too, will always know where they came from and that they were loved."

Jack sipped his beer. Was that too much information? And yet after the week he'd had, sitting here, tipping back while Dave philosophized on the context of family seemed somehow acceptable. Even agreeable.

It was good to truly shirk off the Lassiter problem for a while. To forget how upset Becca had still been when he'd dropped her home. No matter how combustible the chemistry—no matter how much Becca had wanted what they'd shared—he couldn't believe she would ever want to lay eyes on him again. How could something so good end up so bad?

"You grew up an only child, right?" Dave was saying.

"My mother had health problems. My parents rated it a small miracle that I was conceived."

Jack always felt a kind of bond between Ellie Lassiter and his own mother because of that.

"Did you ever wonder what it would be like to have a sister or brother?"

Funny he should ask. "One of my first memories was asking my dad if he could stop on his way home from work and pick one up for me."

They both chuckled. Jack was enjoying the downtime, but he supposed it wouldn't do to get *too* friendly. He needed to wrap things up and get back on the road soon.

"Dave, I've been thinking about our deal. I'd like to throw a bit more into the hat."

Jack offered a figure—more than he'd even intended. When Dave simply sat there studying him with the hint of a smile on his lips, Jack shifted in his seat, cleared his throat. Perhaps he needed to clarify his position.

"I like you, Dave. You're a stand-up guy. But I'm not looking at this with the prospect of becoming business partners."

"You're not."

"No, I'm not."

"How about brothers?"

Jack's stomach knotted but he held his gaze. "I'm sorry. I can't become part of your family."

"You already are."

Jack breathed slowly out. Okay, this was getting awkward. He pushed to his feet. "I should head off."

Dave remained seated. "I'd rather you stay. We still have so much to talk about."

When Dave's oddly calm expression held, Jack confronted him. Something more than a business deal was going on here. "What's this all about?"

"I told you—"

"Family?"

"I only found out two months ago."

"Found out *what?*"

"Two months ago, my mother was in hospital. Complications with diabetes. She passed away."

Jack exhaled. What was he supposed to say to that? He lowered his voice. "I'm sorry. My own mother died ten years ago."

She'd been a loving, selfless person. Jack had shed tears at her funeral and wasn't ashamed to admit it. He was shell-shocked when his father had followed her only months later.

"Before she died," Dave went on, "she said she needed to pass something on. A story about me that also involves you, Jack."

"You're not making any sense."

"Your father never knew…"

For God's sake. "Spit it *out.*"

"Your father dated my mother when she originally lived in Cheyenne. They had a disagreement and broke up. It seemed his family didn't think she was good enough. Not long after that, he married your mother and my mom moved and married my dad." He sat back. "She didn't want her new husband to know that she was pregnant with John Reed's baby. That she was three months pregnant with me."

As Jack's ears began to ring, he simply stared and then coughed out a mirthless laugh. "You want me to believe…what? That I have a half brother…that you're my half brother and my father hid it from me my entire life?"

"He never knew."

Jack's ears and brow were burning. *What a crock.* There wasn't a single memory that so much as hinted that any of it was true. David Baldwin needed his head examined if he thought for one moment he would swallow this. Jack ought to walk away from the whole deal right now.

"For decades my mother followed your family's lives," Dave went on. "She particularly followed your accomplishments, Jack."

"Why are you doing this?"

"Because I want to make up for all those lost years. I thought you might want the same."

Jack wanted to tell him to get a grip on reality. But the emotion shining in Dave's eyes stopped him. It was affection. Compassion.

Brotherly love?

Jack collapsed back into the chair. After he drained that beer, he squeezed the empty in his hand and groaned out, "I'll need another drink."

Dave pushed to his feet, headed for the bar. "I'll make it Scotch."

Thirteen

Becca was gutted when Angelica Lassiter's press conference didn't take place. It didn't take her much to guess who had swooped in and got to J.D.'s haunted daughter before she could make any kind of announcement.

Catching up with a friend about the upcoming wedding, Felicity was in town again. When Fee arrived on her doorstep that evening, Becca was pretty much over the whole Lassiter mess. Over pretty much everything. For the first time in her life, she wanted to crawl in a hole and not bother coming back out.

As she opened the door, Fee simply stood there, looking disappointed and confused. Becca had kept her emotions under tight rein these past hours. Now despair rose in her throat, choking off air. Becca felt so miserable, she could only shrug and murmur, "Guess you heard."

The world must know by now…Jack Reed and Becca "Brainless" Stevens had blown off L.A. to get it on. And not in some motel room. Out in the great outdoors.

Shoot me now.

"I won't waste time asking if it's true," Fee said.

"I haven't seen the photos." Becca *never* wanted to see them. Never mind anyone else's opinions—what would her parents say?

In her favorite Raiders jersey and thick comfort socks, Becca led her friend through to the kitchen where Fee presented a bottle of red wine.

"Thought you might need a drink," she said. "I know I do."

"That'll go perfectly with the cheesecake."

Becca had already eaten half of it—the remaining half sat on the counter, next to a used plate.

Fee looked stupefied. "Tell me you didn't eat all that in one afternoon."

"It was a piece of cake." Becca gave her friend a withering grin. "That was a joke."

"Sorry," Fee said, "but you don't look like you've been yucking it up."

"Getting high on sugar is better than slitting my wrists."

"Don't talk like that. Nothing's ever that bad. Even this."

Becca thought of all the kids at risk of self-harm and suicide and flinched, ashamed. Of course, Fee was right. Nothing was worth taking your own life. That didn't mean that she didn't feel like hell.

Fee found two goblets while Becca cracked open the Merlot. She poured two generous servings and proposed a toast.

"To the world's weakest woman," Becca said and downed a mouthful.

Fee refrained. "Maybe alcohol isn't a good idea right now."

"Liquor has never been my problem." At the moment, nagging self-pity was.

"You are *anything* but weak."

"Except where Jack is concerned."

"Honey, forgive me for saying, but you're not alone there."

Good friends were always honest, and Fee was right on the money. She wasn't Jack's first conquest and she wouldn't be his last. One more notch on the bedpost.

"I knew Jack's reputation with women. He's a lady-killer. He wouldn't deny it. That's what my brain says. Then my heart got mixed up somewhere along the way and, suddenly, somehow, he looked like Prince Charming. It's crazy, but there's something about his voice—about his *everything*—that drags me in. I thought I could control it."

Fee narrowed her eyes. "You haven't fallen in love with him, have you?"

"Is falling in lust any better?" Becca set down her glass and covered her flushed face with her hands. "What am I going to do?"

Taking a hold of an arm, Fee hauled Becca over to the breakfast nook and sat her down.

"First you need to know that you have a lot of friends at Lassiter Media," she said, sitting down, too. "People who won't throw you under a bus, no matter what. But, yeah, this doesn't look good. I can't see Evan McCain being so understanding."

"Evan and I spoke. He wasn't pleased, to say the least. He knows I had all the right intentions. It was my execution that was off."

Whenever Becca thought about facing her coworkers' disappointed faces—their curious glances—she shuddered.

"I'd already arranged to have the rest of the week off." And she hadn't had a vacation break since starting at the foundation, so there were days up her sleeve. "Evan suggested I go back into the office Monday. I guess he'll have figured out what to do with me by then."

"And Jack Reed?" Fee asked.

Just the sound of his name sent her blood pounding. "I would be happy if I never had to see that sexy, bloodsucking smile ever again."

Fee arched a brow. "So, you're not in love with the man? You kind of skated around that question earlier."

Becca crossed to the counter and forked cheesecake into her mouth. It didn't hit the spot. Didn't ease the pain.

"I wish I'd never laid eyes on him," she said, avoiding the question again. "I wish I could go back and erase everything that's happened this past week."

"So, when he calls—and he *will* call—you're unavailable? It's just I know what you're going through. Being a slave to your own emotions, wishing you could feel differently but not being able to get past the longing. It's all consuming. An irritating, breathtaking reality that just won't go away."

Understanding, Becca smiled softly. "You went through that with Chance."

"Oh, yeah. In the end, my surrender set me free."

"You're saying that I should, what? Follow my heart where Jack is concerned?" Becca shivered even as added warmth swirled through her veins at the thought of being with him again. "He's nothing like Chance Lassiter."

"But you're not attracted to Chance. For all his apparent faults, you're attracted to Jack." Fee joined her friend by the counter. "Have you asked yourself why you're so angry right now?"

"I know why. I allowed this to happen."

"You mean you couldn't *stop* it from happening."

Fee didn't get it. There was such a thing as responsibility. "I know you must be feeling like all the world is filled with roses and love songs right now. I am so, so happy for you and Chance. But there is no way this side of forever that Jack and I will ever end up a happy couple. We have less than nothing in common. I despise what he stands for. His antics with Angelica have done so much damage to the foundation, and he couldn't care less."

Fee took a few seconds and then cocked her head. "As hard as it is, I think you ought to force yourself to look at those pictures of you and Jack in that lake."

The thought of thousands ogling those ultraprivate moments made Becca want to puke. Or was that the cheesecake?

"They must be plastered all over the internet by now."

"To my mind," Fee went on, "they show two people who look as if they belong with one another. Call me Cupid, but I don't think you and Jack are done just yet."

There were two reasons Jack tucked in his tail and went home to Cheyenne.

First, he needed time and space to absorb what he'd learned from David Baldwin. Dave believed that he and Jack were half brothers…that they shared a biological father. Dave had finished by saying that, if Jack agreed, he wanted to provide DNA material for testing.

Jack's first thought had been that it was some kind of scam meant to glean or extort money. His second thought was to wonder how his life might change if Dave's theory were true. He had no aunts or uncles. Since his parents had passed away, no extended family at all.

Although he'd never dwelled on it, Jack had always felt a sense of aloneness most during holidays. Everyone had somewhere to go Christmas day. He worked his private life so that he wasn't short on invitations. But even at his age, Christmas without family felt kind of hollow. A nonevent.

Waiting for the DNA results was harder than Jack had imagined. Anticipation was made worse by the second reason he'd left L.A. Jack hated how he and Becca had parted company. He had hurt her, embarrassed her, and he cared too damn much to ever want to risk doing that again. That meant staying the hell away.

And so he'd gone to bunk down in the place he'd once called home.

The single-story ranch-style house was modest compared to some of the neighboring places. Certainly a far cry from the luxury of either of his L.A. abodes. But when he set his bags down inside his childhood bedroom and looked around at the high school pennants on the wall and his first CD player, Jack felt a sense of peace…grounded in a way he could never be in California.

He simply chilled for the first couple of days. The freezer was stocked and the fridge had enough beer to last. By the third day, he got itchy feet. He revved up the ten-year-old pickup his dad had left in the garage. Slapping a Stetson atop his head, Jack drove north, headed for the Big Blue.

Thirty miles on, the famous ranch came into view. Originally two hundred acres, the Big Blue now encompassed 30,000 acres, breeding Wyoming's most sought after Hereford cattle. J.D.'s nephew Chance resided in the original ranch house. The main house where Chance's mother lived was an 11,000-square-foot two-story structure made of hand-cut logs and wood shingles, built when Ellie and J.D. had adopted the boys. Many times Jack and J.D. had taken brandy out on the flagstone deck, off from the great room, to discuss sport and finance. That seemed so long ago now.

Jack sat outside the gates with the truck idling for a full five minutes. He'd come to fill a curiosity and see the Big Blue again, but he had no intention of paying a call. He wouldn't be welcome, not like in the old days when he had been viewed a friend of the family rather than foe— Angelica being the current exception, of course.

Maybe he'd go visit Logan downtown. The ambitious attorney and he might not be buddies, as such, but at least

Logan understood Jack's current situation with regard to Lassiter Media like no one else could.

Jack was ready to perform a U-turn when another, newer truck pulled into the wide driveway. When Jack recognized the driver, he wound down his window, as did she.

"How you doing, Marlene?"

"I'm real good, Jack. You coming inside?"

Marlene had turned sixty this year. She wore her brown hair in a short, no-nonsense style. Her hazel eyes were round and kind. After her husband had died twenty-four years ago, she'd moved in here from the original house to take care of J.D.'s children. Rumor said that she also cared for J.D. in a wifely fashion. More power to 'em.

"I was on my way into town," he let her know.

"Gonna grab a steak from the Grill?"

And risk seeing Dylan if he was in town? Not likely.

"I was going to stop by Logan Whittaker's office."

"Give him my regards." Marlene propped an elbow on the window ledge. "I sure don't like the position J.D.'s will has put you boys in."

Jack appreciated her concern but this was neither the time nor place to get into it. "It'll all work out," he assured her.

She leaned in closer and lowered her voice as if someone might overhear. "I know what this is about. At least, living with J.D. and his concerns, I'm pretty sure I know."

Jack took a moment and then smiled. He wondered if Marlene had worked it out, or whether J.D. had mentioned something before that final fatal night when he collapsed at Angelica and Evan's wedding rehearsal dinner. Either way, at this point in time, Jack was under obligation to keep quiet. If things unraveled the way he believed they would, the true nature of the part he had played in this tug-of-war would be revealed soon enough.

What would Becca say?

"J.D. was a good daddy," Marlene said. "He loved his princess more than anyone. More than anything. I'm glad she has a good friend to look after her now that he's gone."

That touched Jack in a way he hadn't anticipated. He was used to being viewed in a far less positive light. His mother had always said a kind word went a long way.

Sitting back, Marlene put her truck into gear. "Take care, Jack. Be sure and come back when this is all over."

For Jack, that couldn't be soon enough.

David Baldwin contacted Jack at the end of that week. The results were in and they confirmed his suspicion. When Jack heard, he flew back to L.A. and went directly to his brother's house.

He met the kids—Jack's very own nieces and nephews—and then enjoyed a big family meal of mashed potatoes and meat loaf in a room full of conversation and laughter and so much…well, *love.* By the end of the evening, he'd accepted that these people were indeed family. He planned to get to know them all a whole lot better.

Saying good-night on the front porch, Jack wanted his brother to know one important thing.

"I'm not upset with your mother for keeping her secret all those years. I get she was only trying to protect the people she cared about most."

"I'm sorry I never met your father." Dave eased into that familiar lopsided smile. "*Our* father. I wish we'd had the chance to know one another."

Those thoughtful eyes, his warm laugh… "Dad was a lot like you, you know."

Dave's eyebrow's lifted. "Really?"

Jack brought his brother close for a man hug. In some ways, this news was like receiving a gift from beyond the grave. The opposite of Angelica's situation.

When her father had died, she'd received what might equate to a kick in the pants. But the show wasn't over yet. Jack still hoped it would all work out for her, even if that meant it wouldn't work out for him. He'd like to believe that discovering that he had a brother—family—had changed his view on how he conducted business. In one important way, it had: he wouldn't be taking over and ransacking Dave's company. Other plans were in store there. Family was family.

He would not, however, reconsider his move on Lassiter Media. Evan McCain had cemented his stand and Jack Reed was standing by his. He had no choice.

Jumping in his car, Jack switched on his phone. Angelica had left a message asking him to call her as soon as possible. She answered on the first ring.

"How was Cheyenne?" she asked.

"Quiet."

He had let her know before leaving where he'd be. He could have been back in L.A. if she'd needed him here within a couple of hours.

"How's things with you?"

He heard her draw down a breath. "I had planned to speak to you in person about this…you've done so much to try to help. But there's really no need for you to waste time coming over."

He braced himself. "I'm listening."

"I've decided I'm going to step back."

Jack's chin went up. "Go on."

"I can't do it. I *won't* do it. My family means more to me than raging or crying over something I thought should be mine."

"Angelica—"

"No, Jack. Not this time. Let me finish. Dad was the smartest man I've ever known. I loved him. I respected him. It's time for me to make peace with his final wishes, with my family but, most of all, with myself. It's over. I'm backing away from the fight."

He waited before replying, "In the end, that's your decision."

"I'm glad you understand. And there's one more thing."

"Anything I can do to help."

"I want you to know that if you ever try to take over Lassiter Media anytime in the future, I'll do everything in my power to make certain that you fail. So will my brothers."

Jack rapped his fingertips on the steering wheel. "And Evan?"

"As long as Evan is the CEO of Lassiter Media, I will support him in that capacity."

A smile eased across Jack's face even as he kept his tone solemn. "Is there any way I can convince you to reconsider?"

"Nothing in this world you or anyone else can say will change my mind."

As soon as she disconnected, he put through a call to Logan. The attorney sounded apprehensive.

"I'm hoping this is good news," Logan said.

"The *best*."

Logan's voice dropped. "Are you saying what I think you're saying?"

"I just got off the phone from Angelica. She's made up her mind. She's throwing in the towel. Tossing it away for good."

"There's no way to talk her around?"

"None."

"You're certain?"

"To quote Angelica, it's over." Smiling, Jack shut his eyes and dropped his head back on the rest. *And thank God for that.*

* * *

As soon as Jack Reed appeared, his impressive physique filling the doorway of her office, Becca shot to her feet.

Today she had returned to work. It had been difficult facing her co-workers. Even harder would be her scheduled appointment to meet with Evan later in the day. She was prepared for the worst. If she were in his position, regardless of any good intentions, she would throw herself out the door.

Now that time had passed since that last incident outside of Hailey's café, she'd assumed that Jack had swept her from his mind. Trust him to show up here, at the Lassiter Media Building, and make a big performance. Did the man have no shame? Did he not care at all about her future? Her feelings?

As he shut her office door, Becca backed up a step. "How did you get in here?"

"Security downstairs was either asleep or didn't recognize my mug shot. I made my own way from this floor's reception area. I think your cohorts were all too stunned to stop or question me. Not that it would have done any good if they'd tried."

She snatched up her phone extension at the same time she told him in a firm clear voice, "Kindly leave."

If he wouldn't go, she would call security. The police. Hell, she'd bring in the National Guard if she had to. Word would have reached Evan. If her goose hadn't been cooked here before now…

"You need to hear what I have to say," Jack said, striding over to join her behind her desk. "You'll want to crack open a bottle of champagne when I'm through."

She was shaking inside and out. "I'll say it one more time. Leave, Jack. Leave now before this turns ugly."

Like the last time they'd seen each other. She loathed recalling how the reporter had smirked at their predicament that afternoon. Only now, with Jack standing so close, more pleasant memories began to rise to the surface, like how incredible and secure those strong arms had felt whenever he'd held her. Without meaning to, she breathed in his scent and suddenly she was reliving the heat she'd enjoyed whenever his mouth had claimed hers.

But all that was past. She had washed her hands of him. Nothing could make her want to go through that torment again. Not even that heart-thumping, devilish grin.

"I do wish you wouldn't smile at me like that," she said, turning away and punching that call through to security.

Reaching over, he took the receiver and dropped it back in its cradle.

She blinked at him. "Excuse me? You can't just waltz in here and tell people they need to listen to you. You don't own the place yet."

"Looks like I won't own it anytime in the future, either." His eyes shone down into hers as he edged nearer still. "Will I order up the ice bucket now?"

The floor tilted beneath Becca's feet. She had to unravel her arms and lean against the desk before her knees gave way. Was she reading this right?

"You mean…there's not going to be a takeover?" He'd stepped back from helping Angelica in her fight to take over Lassiter Media? No. Surely that was too easy. Too good to be true. Becca looked at him through narrowed eyes and took two full steps back.

"I don't believe you."

"You don't have to. I have no doubt it'll make this evening's news."

She waited, listening to her pulse beat in her ears. He wasn't laughing. Wasn't lying?

"You mean it?"

"Every word."

As reality sank in, happy tears welled in her eyes. Un-imaginable pressure lifted off her shoulders. "When...?"

"Angelica and I spoke last night."

A laugh escaped from Becca's lips. She wrapped her arms around his neck and laughed some more. He felt so solid. So reliable and, at the end of it all, understanding. She wanted to kiss him until their lips were bruised.

Then she remembered Angelica. As much as Becca wanted this outcome for so many reasons, poor Angelica must be feeling gutted. Jack was her last hope of regaining control of this company.

She stepped back but held his right hand in both of hers. "How did Angelica take it? She must be upset."

"It was Angelica's call. Not mine."

"Oh?" Okay. That made a difference. "Did you try to talk her out of it?"

"Of course I tried. But this time there was no turning back. She'd made up her mind to put family first, corporate aspirations second."

Becca dropped his hand.

"You mean she's just giving up...walking away from the fight?" *And no thanks to you?*

When he nodded, Becca gathered herself. Those warm fuzzy feelings cooled. Other less favorable feelings were taking their place. Suddenly Jack didn't look so reliable.

"Well, I know why I'd want champagne, but you tried to talk her out of it." *And not for the first time.* "Why are you so happy?"

"It's really quite simple." Jack leaned back against the desk, crossed his ankles then his arms. "J.D. always meant for Angelica to run Lassiter Media, but he didn't want her to make the same mistakes he'd made."

"What are you talking about?"

"J.D. devoted all his time and energy to business, right?"

"Right."

"Corporate matters overshadowed every facet of his life. After the first heart attack, when Angelica stepped up to the plate, she became so engrossed in work, J.D. became worried that, when he went, his daughter would leave behind everything, including family, in the pursuit of corporate power."

Jack caught Becca's hand and drew her over to the couch.

"She did seem totally committed," Becca said, sitting down beside him.

"When J.D. made changes to his will in those final months, he also had a secret codicil drawn up. Logan Whittaker and I were the only ones who knew it existed. If and when Angelica accepted the will's terms and supported the family and Evan going forward, it would trigger the codicil. She would then be awarded controlling voting interest in Lassiter Media, which had been J.D.'s wish all along."

Had he said this was simple? "Only when she accepted the terms of the will…?"

"The way J.D. saw it, Angelica needed to understand and appreciate the importance of family first and foremost. He wanted her to run the company but, above all else, he wanted her to enjoy the rewards of a balanced life."

Becca slumped back. Poor Angelica. She thought she understood now what J.D. had been trying to accomplish, but what a test! Not only had it driven a wedge between Angelica and her brothers, she had gone to war with a man she had wanted to marry. If J.D. had wanted his daughter to embrace the benefits of family, to Becca's mind, he'd gone about it in a weird way.

"You were part of this scheme?" she asked.

"It was my job to push her as hard as I could in the other direction."

"Toward a hostile-takeover bid? That's…*twisted*."

"J.D.'s plan, not mine. He wanted her to struggle with t, if necessary. He wanted her to be sure."

"J.D. probably expected Angelica to be married before ne died and the will went into effect. Did he consider the stress it would bring to Angelica's marriage to Evan?" She thought for a moment. "Or did he want to test the honesty of Evan's intentions somehow, too?"

"I only know he chose me to push the barrel."

"He obviously thought you were the man for the job." As unbelievable as it seemed, the plans and its resolution were sinking in. Jack hadn't been the bad guy in all this drama. He'd been a *good* guy willing to *look* like the bad guy. Which made him *extra* good.

He hadn't planned to steal from the rich to give to the poor exactly, but neither had he plotted to trick Angelica into a takeover and then sell off the pieces under her feet. For Jack, that was big. Heck, it was huge!

Becca's smile stretched from ear to ear. If Jack felt relieved, she felt euphoric!

Falling forward, she planted a closed-mouth kiss on his lips. "Sorry. I'm just so happy this nightmare has turned out so well. Angelica gets control of her company."

"Don't apologize." Tipping close, he brushed his lips over hers. "Best part is, when word gets out, any negative publicity the foundation has weathered will be reversed."

"But Evan…"

"He gets a big payout."

"I don't know how much compensation would be enough for losing this company *and* the woman he loved. Maybe still loves."

Jack tried to sound convincing. "Evan will bounce back."

"And you…do you know what you are?" She cupped his jaw and then grazed her thumb over the stubble of his chin. "You're a hero."

He drew back a little. "I was only following instructions."

"I wish I'd known."

"I wish I could have told you."

Her heart was throbbing, aching in her throat. God, his lips looked good. And now it didn't matter who took their picture. The truth was out and her Jack was back.

As her palm trailed down his shirt, she shifted closer still. His body heat steamed through his shirt, warming her all over, making her sigh.

"So, what are you doing now?"

His lips brushed hers as he answered, "I'm kidnapping you."

"A copycat strategy. I like it." She squeezed his thigh and thought to add, "Not that I'm in favor of the general nature of your business."

"The corporate-raiding stuff. Then you might like my other news. But I'm afraid it'll take most of the day to relay every detail, so you might want to inform your assistant that you'll be unavailable."

When he kissed her again, deeply this time, the fireflies humming around in her stomach began to burst into flame.

Coming up for air, she murmured, "Should we leave a ransom note?"

"Let's say, *gone fishing*."

Thirty minutes later, they were naked in his bed.

Fourteen

He and Becca walked out of that office and away from the Lassiter Media Building without a care in the world.

Or it sure had seemed that way at first.

Jack had hoped that Becca would take his news concerning Angelica well. He had wondered whether she might have struggled with believing him. He'd imagined her telling him to leave and not come back even after the facts had been verified. He'd been pleasantly surprised, to say the least, when she'd accepted the truth so readily. He had read her eyes, her body language, in those first moments when she'd been trying so hard to hate him.

In reality, she missed him, like an addict missed her drug. He knew because he felt the same way. All the pieces had fallen into place. This morning, he'd arranged for his bank to wire a sizable sum to the Lassiter Charity Foundation—specifically to help Brightside House and its endeavors. It was a good cause. And there was the added benefit of making Becca happy, because when she was happy, he was happy. Happier than he'd ever been.

He took her to his penthouse and let a valet park his car while he grabbed Becca's hand and rushed her to his private elevator. As soon as the metallic door whirred open and he had her inside, alone, he gathered her close, grazed his palms up and down the back of her red designer dress and forced himself to wait a moment more.

"You're more beautiful than I remembered."

She fanned her fingers over his chest, watching the action before looking up at him from beneath her lashes. "Aren't you going to kiss me?"

He gripped her tush and drove her hips against him. She laughed and then coiled her arms around his neck. With those killer heels, she was the right height to feel *just* how much he wanted to kiss her.

"If I start here and now," he growled against her lips, "we might be riding this elevator all day."

"So?" She tilted her head. "You own the building, don't you?"

Good point.

His mouth was one thumping heartbeat away from taking hers when the doors whirred open. He swept her up into his arms and strode to the center of the living room.

"Do you have a Merv here?" she asked.

"There's just the two of us."

The morning light flooding in through the wall-to-wall windows caught a flicker of unease in her eyes. "No cameras?"

He lifted her until the tips of their noses touched. "We have nothing to be ashamed of. Do you hear me?"

"I hear you. That's all behind us now."

So true. He did have some additional news to share, but it could wait.

He kissed her, lightly at first, a feathery brush of lips.

The contact sent rounds of pleasure ricocheting throughout his veins. Then he covered her mouth with his completely and leaned in as those sensations fired harder, longer. A thousand times deeper.

They had until morning. By then everyone would know that Evan was out, Angelica was in and Becca would need to attend to issues stemming from the switch. But what he would give to convince her to take a week or two leave. So they could spend every moment in bed.

With his mouth working over hers—while she was still in his arms—he crossed to the corridor that led to the master suite. He set her down at the foot of the bed and ran his hands up her back. With his brow resting on hers, he drew the zipper of her dress all the way down and then slipped it off her arms. Red linen rustled and fell around her feet.

He hadn't meant to get hung up at this point, but that lingerie was ten miles past sexy. He took a step back to get a better look. With a sultry grin, she cocked one hip and set her hands on her hips.

"You like?"

"You love to mix it up as far as office attire is concerned, don't you?" he asked, taking in the provocative picture from top to toe. "One day jeans, the next…" He wagged a finger. "What exactly do you call those things?"

"A garter slip. Satin and mesh." She performed a slow turn. "The color is raspberry."

He moved close again, letting his palms drift over the curvy satin all the way down to the strip of firm flesh left bare at the top of each thigh. A hand-span below that, the bands of her silk stockings began. He grazed his jaw lightly up one side of her cheek and then scooped her hair aside. Sliding the strap of her garter slip off a shoulder, he lowered his mouth to that smooth sweep of skin. She smelled fresh and…the only word that fit was *classy*. He ran the tip of his tongue along the ledge joining shoulder to neck then all the way up the side of her throat. He felt her shiver, a delicious, delicate quiver that only cranked the heat up all the more.

"Take off your shirt," she murmured. "Sit on the edge of the bed."

He nipped her earlobe. "You like to be the boss?"

"I'd like to take turns."

Jack had no objection to letting her go first.

He backed up toward the bed, at the same time releasing the buttons on his cuffs and shirt front. He took a seat while Becca made a tantalizing show of slipping down the second shoulder strap. After slipping off her shoes, she strolled forward and lifted her leg, setting her foot on the quilt next to his thigh. She flicked the stocking snap and leaned forward. Using her palms, she rolled the silk all the way down.

Jack was torn—should he look at that scrumptious toned leg or the closer, perhaps even more tempting view of her breasts wanting to spill out of their low-cut bra cups? Then there was the glimpse he'd caught of her panties when she'd switched legs to lower her other stocking.

He wound out of his shirt and tossed it on the floor. Then he reached for her hands but her fingers slipped through his as she moved back, a grin on her face.

Happy to play, he leaned back on his hands while she caught the hem of her slip and eased the satin up over her belly, ribs, breasts, until she stood holding the slip in one hand, wearing only panties.

The room's shutters were slanted, letting in strips of light that highlighted parts of her beautiful body. She moved forward with so much poise and confidence, Jack's anticipation turned a cartwheel and ramped up again. It had near killed him to keep away these past days. But the wait had been worth every minute.

He heeled off his shoes and got rid of his pants, briefs

and socks before she'd closed the distance and crawled up onto his lap. As she tasted his lips, she used her weight to ease him down onto his back. Straddling him, she kissed him deeply. Her arms curled around his head while her breasts brushed over his chest. When she tried to draw away, he gripped the top of her arms to bring her back. She only laughed and slid down the length of his body. Her lips trailed his throat, the center of his chest, over the ruts of his abs....

Then her tongue was looping a slow, purposeful circle around his navel, setting off a series of fireworks. His fingers filed through her hair as his hips rocked up.

She slid down more until the seam of her lips skimmed the tip of his erection. He felt her fingers wrap around the base of his shaft, squeeze and then drag up at the same time her amazing mouth went down.

He gripped the quilt and grit his teeth. This was scorching, intense. He could feel the beginnings of a climax burning, begging for release. He focused on the sublime rhythm she'd created, the tow of her hand working in perfect sync with the pump and pull of her mouth. Her other hand was spread over his chest, rhythmically kneading one side like a kitten preparing its bed.

As her mouth drew away, cooler air met warm wet flesh. It was a good thing she stopped when she did. He'd almost forgotten how much he wanted to satisfy her rather than the other way around. He caught her around the waist as she straightened. Then he cupped her breasts, grazing palms over distended nipples. He slid a hand down the front of her panties. She was swollen, wet. As ready as he was.

He urged her over onto her back and dropped a line of slow, moist kisses around each breast before angling lower. He hooked a finger into the side of her panties' crotch, pulled aside the satin and tenderly kissed her there. He heard her sigh before she arched into his caress. He tasted her again, relishing the scent and feel of her beneath his lips before he whipped off her last scrap of clothing and found a condom in a drawer.

When he was sheathed, he joined her again. She felt warm and soft and her eyes held nothing but trust. He positioned himself between her thighs while she ran her fingers through his hair.

He felt as if a furnace were burning inside of him. Her brow and the valley between her breasts were damp, too. He pushed inside of her, closing his eyes and tilting his face toward the ceiling as he buried himself to the hilt.

Her legs coiled around the back of his and she whispered to him how wonderful he felt, how she never wanted this to end. He built the friction as they moved together until he felt as if he was a part of her and she a part of him.

He was aware of her inner walls squeezing, of her fingers digging into his shoulders and her head rocking back. He watched the line crease between her brows, studied the smile lifting the corners of her parted lips. As he upped the tempo and force of each thrust, he felt her panting breath warm on his face. He lowered his mouth close to hers at the same time her legs clamped down hard.

Then he closed his eyes and held her tight as they both let go at once.

Fifteen

"You're not going to believe this," Becca said, gaping at a message on her smartphone.

Jack rolled over and stole another glorious morning kiss and then murmured against her lips, "You've decided you want to order in Danishes?"

"All my cravings have been well and truly satisfied." She tasted his lips again then amended, "For now."

They had stayed in Jack's penthouse the entire day *and* night. They'd ordered in dinner and had devoured barbecue ribs and butter pecan ice cream sitting out on the balcony, their feet propped up on the railing. Around ten, they'd fallen asleep on a soft-as-clouds leather lounge while they watched *Forrest Gump*. An hour ago they'd taken a long, sudsy shower together before Jack had dialed up the AC and pulled her under his duck-down duvet.

Becca hadn't checked back in with Sarah. Worse, she'd turned off her phone until now. She'd had an amazing time playing hooky with her bad boy, but it seemed lots had happened while she'd been away.

"Sarah says word is out about Angelica being reinstated as CEO. With you out of the picture, donations are already pouring back in." She sent Jack a sympathetic look. "No disrespect intended."

"None taken." He snuggled into her neck, tickling and arousing her as he nuzzled. "And so, all is right with the world."

Sighing, she beamed up at the ceiling while he nibbled her shoulder. "This has all turned out so well. I'm waiting for the bubble to burst."

He looked into her eyes. A soft, sexy smile tugged one corner of his mouth. "I guess sometimes there are happy endings."

"I guess there really are."

He kissed her again, long and slow and deep, before sitting up against the headboard alongside of her. "What are you doing Thanksgiving?"

"Are you asking me on a date?" she teased.

"I'm not sure. Is a family occasion classified as a date?"

"You don't have any family."

"As of yesterday, I officially do."

He passed on everything that had happened between himself and David Baldwin this past week. Jack Reed had a brother? Nieces and nephews?

"My God, Jack. That's *fantastic*. Why didn't you tell me sooner?"

"I wanted this other Lassiter stuff to be settled first." He lifted her hand and dropped a kiss on the underside of her wrist. "One victory at a time."

"You're not an only child anymore. How does it feel? Amazing, right?"

"The truth?"

"Of course."

"It feels almost too good." He leaned in to kiss her shoulder. "Like it feels almost too good to be holding you again."

She moved to run her fingers through his hair. "We should accept good things when they come our way."

"I'm beginning to understand that."

Their next kiss felt like the first of all their tomorrows. Which was thinking too fast, too soon. But she couldn't help wanting to take a hold of this fantasy and actually believe they could live it.

As the kiss broke, she curled into his arm and leaned her cheek against his chest.

"So, what's happening with your brother's business?" she asked.

"Take a guess."

"You're going to become partners."

"Uh-huh."

Her jaw dropped. "You're kidding."

"I offered to gift him the funds. He refused. Then he put it in a way I couldn't turn my back on. He said that through no fault of our own we were separated. Now it was within our power to be close, and stay close. Working together, becoming partners, would mean we'd be in touch most days, not just holidays. He doesn't want to simply maintain the connection. He wants to build on it. So do I."

"You're really going to be building a company up?" She laughed. "Call a medic!"

He tickled her until she begged him to stop.

"It's time we got something clear," he said, bundling her up in those big beautiful arms again. "I may make money out of applying a keen business eye to enterprises that can provide a larger profit operating as smaller entities."

"Say that again slowly."

"That does not, however, make me Scrooge."

"I know, I know. You give to charity. In fact, Sarah

mentioned in her text that Reed Incorporated had made the biggest of the foundation's recent donations so far." She dropped a kiss on his scratchy chin. "Thank you."

"You're very welcome. And I want you to know that this latest, shall we call it *coming together of minds,* had no influence on the size of that donation. Although, it would be remiss of me not to mention that I am open to bribes."

"Like this?"

She shifted to straddle his lap all the while kissing her way slowly and thoroughly around his neck and chest. He groaned.

"*Exactly* like that. Keep it coming."

As his fingers trailed up and down her back, a thought popped into Becca's head. She'd wondered about it last night halfway through the movie, but it had drifted off again until now. When she felt him growing harder against her belly, she straightened. If she didn't ask this minute, she might never get around to it.

"I'm not sure on one thing," she said, as his palms trailed down her sides.

"What's that?"

"Your job was to keep pushing Angelica toward a take-over bid, right?"

"Right."

He leaned in to draw a nipple into his mouth. She quivered and closed her eyes. It was hard to think straight when he did that.

"You've been actively acquiring shares and positioned your company so it would be ready to move," she said. "I would have thought very soon."

He was running his tongue around her other nipple now. "These things take time."

"It's just…Jack, what would have happened if Angelica hadn't backed down? What if she'd gone ahead with the takeover and you both won?"

"Then she and I would have become partners."

"And you'd have managed all the Lassiter interests together." When he didn't answer, she looked down.

"Jack?"

"We would have worked together, yes."

She waited for him to add something more. Like, *But I would never turn around and do what I've done with every other company I've obtained through fair means or foul.* When nothing came, every hair on her head stood on end. Damn it! She *knew* this was too good to be true.

She shifted off of him and scrunched the duvet up under her arms.

"You were planning to sell off parts of Lassiter Media, weren't you?"

He scratched his head. "I can't say it didn't cross my mind that we could make a huge fortune without a whole lot of work."

"You mean by ripping apart someone else's work of a lifetime."

"There would have been discussions."

Oh, come on. "Angelica is no match for you."

"You've said that before but what about the way she stood up to me yesterday? Her father would have been proud."

Becca's throat was aching now. Suddenly she felt empty. Betrayed. Or was that merely foolish?

"You would have made it difficult, made it ugly, then you would have talked her into folding before the selling price was affected."

"You give me too much credit and Angelica not enough." He sat up straighter.

"What would have happened to the foundation?"

"We would have worked something out there."

"An offer I couldn't refuse?"

"I'm not a criminal, Becca. I'm only being honest with

you. It doesn't matter now because the game is played out and Angelica is where she was always meant to be."

"She'll never know how close she came to bringing it all down on her head."

"And that's the end of it." He reached for her. But his smile didn't look sexy now; she imagined it looked patronizing. Predatory.

She edged away and got to her feet, dragging the duvet along to cover herself. "There is no moving along until we get past this."

"Why worry about something that cannot, will not, happen? This, you and me, we're not about business."

"I know what I'm about. Ethics. Principles. Making the tough decisions so I can wake up in the morning and look at myself in the mirror. Guess what? That's gotten harder since I hooked up with you."

He opened his mouth, shut it again and then stood, too. "Shine a little light on something for me here. You never liked me, and you don't like me now because I'm a selfish, money-hungry, insensitive moron."

"You're not a moron."

"Thanks for clarifying that." He skirted the end of the bed until he stood an arm's length away. "Tell me, how could you lower yourself to sleep with me? And not just once. I must be losing my mind because I thought it was good. *No.* I thought it was *great*. The best."

That took her aback. She struggled for a response.

He moved closer, looming. "You know more about me than anyone. You might not trust me but, damn it, Becca, I trusted you. And for my trouble, you want to rake me over the coals."

She huffed. He would see it that way. "This isn't about you. Not anymore. It's about my feelings, my future, my decisions."

"Right, because my feelings don't count."

"You don't have feelings." She winced. That was going too far. "Or not like you should. If you did, you wouldn't be arguing with me now."

"You think J.D. was an angel?" he drawled. "Do you want to hear about the low deals he cut so that you could crow about all the great works your charity does? There has to be a *take* in order to have a *give*. Someone has to make the money to give it away, and no one makes money, real money, by sitting on a delicate behind letting other people make the choices that need to be made."

She spoke through her teeth, which had to be a damn sight better than speaking through tears. "Don't try to justify your behavior."

"I'm not. I won't. Not to anyone."

She marched toward the bathroom.

He called after her. "Where are you going?"

"Back to reality. *My* reality. Where people own up to their flaws and maybe try to do something about them."

He slapped his thighs. "Right. *Good.* I'm evil because I had good parents, was born with a brain and a drive to succeed."

"You were born with a will to *dominate*."

He shook his head as if he couldn't believe it. "I'm not wrong about most things," he said quietly. "But I was wrong about you."

"You thought you could convert me."

"I thought you could *care* about me." He stabbed a thumb at his chest. "*Me.* Not the money or connections or the name, Jack Reed."

Tears were so close, she could taste them. "Well, whaddya know?" The door swung shut as she finished. "You were wrong!"

Sixteen

"If I'm your sidekick, I hope this doesn't make me Friar Tuck."

Standing at the shooting line on the back lawn of his Beverly Hills house, Jack spun around and frowned. What was Sylvia doing here?

He lowered his bow as she crossed over to join him. She was right to carry her shoes. Those high-priced heels would ruin his lawn—not that he imagined for a minute that had been her motive for taking them off.

"Merv the Man let me through," Sylvia let him know.

"What's up?"

She eyed the distant target. Arrows were scattered all over the place. The bull's-eye, however, remained untouched.

"I was wondering when the boss might be coming back in," she said.

"You don't need help running the office. You have one of the most efficient business minds I know."

"Flattery doesn't work with me, Jackie boy."

"I'm doing other things."

"Like building boats with David Baldwin?"

Sylvia knew that story.

"That's the one good thing to come out of this month's firestorm."

Sylvia offered him a genuine smile. "No one's happier for you than I am."

He redirected his attention to the target. He and Sylvia did bottom-line analysis, not deep and meaningful conversation.

He sucked air in between his teeth. "I have other projects I'm working on."

"Any involve Becca Stevens?"

Eye still on the target, he growled. "No."

"You've been in contact with her, though."

"After I made myself clear, she made herself crystal clear."

In the briefest of summaries, he had also let Sylvia know that, due to the fallout surrounding the twist in J.D.'s will, his and Becca's "challenge" had come to an acrimonious end. He hadn't given up the finer details.

"I admitted to her that I would have followed through with the Lassiter Media takeover if Angelica hadn't changed her mind."

Of course, Sylvia didn't look the least bit surprised. "And since she ditched you, you haven't been able to think straight, right?"

"It's a matter of willpower."

He strode back to the line and fired a shot—which sailed over the top.

Damn!

Sylvia crossed over to join him. She took a long moment to study the target.

"Silly idea," she said, "but why don't you call her?"

Don't you know I want to?

"Sometimes in a relationship," he explained, "we say things we don't mean. Words can hurt. They can cut to the bone. But people can apologize, deeply, sincerely, and then get back to the good stuff. Becca and me...we went way beyond that."

Sylvia examined his face, particularly his mouth.

"Wait a minute," she said, and wriggled a finger. "Your bottom lip. Is that a pout? Are you *pouting,* Jack?"

Sylvia was like that. She never let herself, or anyone else on her radar, feel sorry for themselves. She could give a friend money, advice, she would work through the night if a job needed to be done. But no one could ask her for pity.

Jack crossed to the bench and sat down heavily. He swallowed against the lump lodged in his throat and then dealt out the bottom line.

"Becca told me exactly what she thinks of me. I could get over the argument, but she never will. She could never reconcile who she is, what she stands for, with being with a wrecking ball like me."

Sylvia sat down beside him.

"I could chase her," Jack said. "We'd fall into bed again. It'd be good for a while. Then she'd remember who I am, what I've done and the shame would creep back in. The guilt. She'd resent our being together. She'd resent me." He let his bow drop to the ground. "Not a recipe for happiness."

"Sorry," Sylvia said. "I was wrong. I thought you must really care for that woman. I thought she was the reason your schedule has been up the creek and we haven't seen your designer pants in the office for weeks."

"I'm the same Jack Reed," he said. But that was a lie.

"You're hiding."

"I am not *hiding*."

"What are you so afraid of?"

"I'm *not* afraid."

"C'mon. Spit it out."

"No."

"Do it."

Fine! "I'm afraid I'll destroy her. That I'll let her down. I'll let her down and then…" He sighed. "Then I'll have made things even worse. I'm not good at long-term, Sylvia. I'm controlling. I have a controlling personality."

"I bet she'd like the chance to work things out."

His grin was entirely humorless. "I humbly disagree."

"She's taking a sabbatical from the foundation. Rumor is she's going to work in a mission overseas."

"What's the plan, Sylvia? I pack a bag, follow her and we save the world together?"

"I thought you might like to say goodbye at least."

"Why the hell would I want to do that?"

She gave a wry grin. "I've known you to be flippant, ruthless, but never cruel. Never stupid."

"I so don't need this." He pushed to his feet.

She got to hers. "I'm trying to help you."

"I don't need help."

"Everyone needs help sometime, for some reason. Some of us are even big enough to accept it. Don't be a dope. Go to Becca before she leaves, even if she slams the door in your face." She touched his arm, lightly at first and then more firmly. "Take the word of a lonely woman who always needs to be right. Talk to her. You'll regret it if you don't."

Standing on the beach, Becca watched Jack pull up, get out of his car and study Hailey's café before wandering down over the sand to join her.

When she'd answered his call earlier, her hand had shaken, she'd wanted to hang up so bad. But there'd been something different in his voice. Something…real. Had she imagined the self-effacing tone?

It didn't matter now. She'd agreed to meet him. But she had wanted to choose the place. To finish here in Santa Monica on a more adult, less hostile note would bring this episode full circle. And then hopefully she would be able to put aside this constant ache in her chest…in her heart.

She held her breath as he stopped in front of her. In that moment, she saw only his eyes, heard only the waves.

"Where's the Bambino?" he asked.

"I sold it."

"Get outta here. Really?"

"To Hailey's brother."

"Wow. Big step."

"Yeah." She slotted her hands in the front pockets of her denim pedal pushers and dragged a bare foot through the sand. "Moving on."

His smile faded and that different tone she'd heard on the phone was there again.

"Thanks for seeing me," he said.

"Guess you heard about the sabbatical."

He nodded as the wind combed his hair. "Where are you off to?"

"Haven't decided yet."

"The foundation will sure miss you."

Will you miss me, Jack?

She cut off that thought and focused on the ocean until she'd gathered herself again.

"I'm hosting a final auction night next week," she said, speaking to the waves. It hurt too much to look at him here like this. "Then I need time away."

She heard distant barking and turned toward the café. Chichi was scampering down the ramp and onto the sand. He sped right up to Jack, who dropped onto his haunches to play wrestle with him. Becca figured that Chichi would find a stick and the rest of this short time she and Jack had here together would be mediated by this brash third party. Not a bad thing.

But suddenly Chichi turned a tight circle and shot off again. Becca hadn't heard anything, but dogs had good ears; Hailey must have called him back.

"I want you to know," she said, "I'm not angry with you." Not anymore. "In fact, I want to apologize. Being so self-righteous isn't very pretty. I have no right to judge others when my behavior has been less than glowing. I was frustrated." And hurt mostly.

Looking up at her, his dark gaze turned stormy. "Then why are you leaving?"

"I need to work on myself. The best way to do that is to help others. Sort out what's important and what's not." He sat all the way down on the sand, facing the waves with his legs bent, forearms resting on his knees.

"I had a long conversation with a friend," he said. "She thinks we ought to give it a go."

Becca's legs went weak. She'd expected something but nothing as direct as this. After all those nasty things they'd said to each other?

"You and me?" she asked. "Like a *couple?*"

He reached out his hand. She took a hold and knelt beside him, still processing what he'd just said.

"I want us to be together," he went on. "I want to make it work."

She let that sink in. Obviously he didn't know what he was saying.

"What do you mean 'make it work'?"

"I mean negotiate. Compromise. Maybe move in together."

Whoa.

If he wasn't beating around the bush, neither would she.

"Do you want forever?"

A line formed between his brows but he didn't look away.

"That girl I told you about," he said. "I told you I'd proposed. In fact, we were going to be married the next day."

His eyes were reflective now, glassy, like he was living in the past and wasn't in a hurry to come back. Becca felt sick to her stomach. It was bad enough to have a loved one take her own life, but to be faced with that tragedy a day before they were supposed to begin life's most wonderful journey together... *Unimaginable*.

"You still love her," Becca said, wanting to cry for him all these years later.

"She was my best friend." He blinked slowly. "I wonder sometimes if she hadn't met me whether she'd still, you know...be around. The truth is I pushed her too hard. I thought I was helping. So, this is a tough one for me." He blinked a few times as a pulse beat in his jaw. "I want to push you to stay, but there's also that part of me that says— that *always* says—don't try to hold on. It's best to let go."

Becca held her stomach. She didn't think she'd felt so sorry for anyone in her life.

She got to her feet and forced out the words before they got stuck in her throat. "I honestly wish you nothing but happiness."

He looked more resigned than disappointed. "What's happiness? That's the sixty-four-thousand-dollar question."

"It's being at peace with yourself."

Before she walked away, she squeezed his shoulder and prayed that Jack found his.

Seventeen

One week later, Becca was ready to make an announcement.

This Lassiter Charity Foundation Auction Night had been wildly successful, with exceptional items up for grabs and an astounding amount of money having been raised. The high-neck black sheath she wore somehow suited her bittersweet mood. The foundation would not only survive, it would flourish under Angelica's reinstated reign at Lassiter Media. But this was also Becca's last public appearance as director of the Los Angeles-based charity she believed in so much.

A moment ago, Sarah had suggested it was time to offer the guests a final thank-you. Becca had been on her way to the lectern when she'd glimpsed someone standing alone in the back of the ballroom.

He was exceptionally tall with dark hair. His masculine physique was made all the more eye-catching by the tuxedo he wore. As he headed for an exit, she actually considered for a third of one second to simply let him go. However, in her professional capacity here this evening, that wouldn't be right.

Becca wove through the crowd. In her hurry, she bumped into one gentleman's paunch and then immediately knocked darling Mrs. Abernathy and her glass of punch. She apologized profusely to both and kept rushing toward the exit. She caught up the moment the man pushed open the door.

"Jack. *Jack!*"

He turned around. He was so handsome…when he smiled, the entire room seemed to light up.

"I've tried to contact you today," she said. "I spoke to your PA. Jack, I can't thank you enough for your generosity."

"She passed on your invitation. I'm glad the bow and arrowheads brought in a good price."

Good price? More like incredible. "I've never seen such a bidding war. I'm so glad they went to a museum, even if it's overseas."

"I'm glad, too."

They held each other's gazes while music wove through the room and crystal flutes tinkled.

"I'd better let you get back to your guests," he said at last, and turned toward the exit again.

"Wait." She had something she wanted to ask. "Have you heard from Angelica?"

"We spoke today. She's feeling right at home in the CEO's chair. Sage and Dylan are happy for her, too. I'm not sure what's happening with Evan McCain, other than there are rumors he's going to start up his own company with the money J.D. left him via that codicil. Guess he was very generously compensated but he still feels burned by the whole thing."

"It'd be nice if those two got back together. But I understand why she might think Evan somehow conspired with her dad to get controlling interest of the company. That's a lot of hurt to get over on both sides."

"Miracles happen."

When his broad shoulders rolled back and he glanced at the door, she threw in another question.

"How's your brother?"

"We touch base every other day. And I'll see the whole crowd on Turkey Day. And Christmas will be here before you know it. I'll have to do some research on buying gifts for people under sixteen."

"You'll have fun with it."

Sarah appeared at Becca's side.

"Sorry to interrupt. Becca, we need you to announce the total amount that was raised tonight. The mayor's about to leave."

Becca nodded. "I'll be right there."

"Duty calls," Jack said. "Good luck, Becca."

She took a deep breath and let it out on a wistful smile. "Same to you."

When the last of the guests left the ballroom, Sarah gave Becca a congratulatory hug.

"This has to be the most successful fund-raising night in history."

Becca laughed. "I wouldn't go that far."

"I just hate that you're leaving the charity. It's been such a buzz working with you. I've learned so much. But I understand. You have things you need to do. It must be hard leaving, though. Letting go."

"I'll find another job in charity when I get back."

"I mean leaving Jack Reed. You two have some amazing chemistry going on."

Becca hadn't spoken much to Sarah about her dealings with Jack. Of course her assistant had seen those shots taken at the lake…who hadn't? But the look on Sarah's face now—it was as if she believed in fairy dust or something. Real life wasn't like that.

The women said good-night. Sarah had shared a ride with a couple of the other girls from the office. Becca said she'd get a cab home.

Alone in the elevator, Becca hit the button for the ground floor. A moment later, she was crossing the quiet hotel foyer. The click of her heels on the marble tiles echoed through the large glitzy space.

But she didn't want to go home just yet. She wanted to do what she'd never given herself permission to do before: be idle and simply waste time window-shopping on one of the world's most famous streets, Rodeo Drive. It was strange to think that next week it would be a hard task to buy necessities that most people who lived in the States took for granted.

This street was lined with fairy-lit trees and filled with the boutiques of some of the most revered names in the fashion world. She studied the displays, clothes, jewelry, ridiculously priced handbags. And then she came across a window filled with exquisite gowns…beautifully crafted. Most of them were white.

One in particular caught her eye.

The gown was antique-white with a fitting, puff-sleeved satin bodice adorned with a sparkling sea of crystals. The skirt was extra full, flaring from low on the waist. The outer layer was gauzy with a satin band three-quarters down and a floral wreath in the same satin embroidered on the lower front half. It was a reflection of a bygone era when a member of the fairer sex had been encouraged to be fragile and endlessly romantic in the hope of finding her prince.

A dress like that, a dream like that, would need nothing more than the perfect ring. And, needless to say, the perfect groom.

Becca let the illusion wash over her a little more. She saw herself in that gown, her face beaming and eyes filled with love. Beside her stood a man, exceptionally tall, with dark hair, his masculine physique made all the more eye-catching by the tuxedo he wore. And then, the reflection spoke her name. As in…

It *actually* spoke.

Becca spun around. Embarrassment and panic set in so fast, her cheeks caught light. "I thought you'd gone."

Jack only smiled and commented on the window display. "That's some dress."

How must it have looked, her fawning over a whimsical wedding gown alone late at night?

"It's a good street to window-shop," she mumbled.

Jack followed when she set off at a brisk pace, putting the dress behind her.

"I thought it might be something you were thinking of for Felicity's wedding," he said, easily keeping up.

"Oh, she wouldn't have anything so…big."

"Would you?"

She kept her gaze dead ahead. "I might."

"It was very, well, sparkly. I don't think I've seen you wear a piece of jewelry other than a watch."

Slowing her pace, she slid over a defiant look. "I might be saving it all up for one revoltingly gaudy occasion."

"A dress like that would need a pretty impressive ring." He stopped and pulled a small box out of his pocket. "Maybe like this."

As he opened the clasped lid, Becca's jaw dropped. The most amazing piece of jewelry sat glittering up at her from its white satin bed.

"It's sapphires and a pearl." His finger circled the setting. "But you also like diamond and rubies, right?" He pulled out another box. When she stood rigid, overcome with shock, he prodded her. "Go on. Open it."

This couldn't be happening. It felt like everything was moving in a weird kind of slow motion. Someone reached to open the lid. Becca realized it was her. A beautiful white diamond shone up at her. It was mounted in a pool of blood red rubies. Both rings were just as she had imagined they would be way back when she was a girl.

Becca finally formed some words. "Jack…what is this?"

"I want to marry you."

She swallowed against the ache of so many emotions clogging her throat. "We said goodbye…God, I've lost count how many times."

"I worked it out. It's really quite simple. The fact is I love you. And if you love me, why wouldn't we try to work through this…through anything to stay together?" One dark eyebrow lifted as he leaned closer. "You do love me, don't you, Becca?"

Tears stung behind her eyes. No matter how much she tried to hide the truth, everyone else seemed to see it. What was the point in denying it now?

"Of course I love you," she told him. "So much it hurts."

His dark eyes glistened as he gave her a grateful smile. "Let's fix that."

His mouth took hers and, in that instant, sparks tingled and fell through her body. Nothing seemed impossible. She could surmount any problem. Achieve any dream.

When he broke the kiss, Becca felt light-headed, floating, as if her feet no longer touched the ground.

"Are you going to choose?" he asked with his lips still close to hers.

She couldn't argue with him. Not this time. She wanted to say, *I choose you. I choose love.* But he meant the rings. As she looked down to study them again, her vision grew misty with tears. They were both so beautiful. So…*her.*

"I don't think I *can* choose."

"Then you'll have both. As soon as you say yes." He put the boxes in his pocket and drew her close. "I love you, Becca. I want you to be my wife. I don't want to lose you. We *can't* lose each other."

"You really want to do this?" she asked.

"Yeah." He dropped a kiss on her brow and murmured, "I really, really do."

"I have a condition."

He grinned. "Sure."

"That we respect and honor each other for the rest of our lives."

"Just give me the chance."

"We'll both make the rules."

"I only have one."

"Tell me."

After he whispered in her ear, she laughed and wound her fingers into his jacket's lapels. "I think I can handle that." Then she cupped his jaw and fell into a tender gaze that held nothing but adoration for her. "I guess sometimes there really are happy endings."

"Oh, baby." Jack got ready to kiss her again. "Now I know there are."

* * * * *

"**I** shudder to think how far you'd go to get what you wanted."

His expression tightened. "Yeah? Well, we both know how far you'll go, don't we?"

It was a cutting blow. When her father's will left control of Lassiter Media to Evan, it had resulted in an all-out battle between the two of them. Even now, when they both knew it had been a test of her loyalty, their spirits were battered and bruised, their relationship shattered beyond repair.

"I thought I was protecting my family," she defended.

At the time, she couldn't come up with any explanation except that her father had lost his mind, or that Evan had brazenly manipulated J.D. into leaving him control of Lassiter Media.

"You figured you were right and everyone else was wrong?" His steps toward her appeared automatic. "You slept in my arms, told me you loved me, and then accused me of defrauding you out of nearly a billion dollars."

All the pieces had added up in her mind, and they had been damning for Evan. "Seducing me would have been an essential part of your overall plan to steal Lassiter Media."

"Shows you how little you know about me."

"I guess it does."

Even though she was agreeing, the answer seemed to anger him.

"You *should* have known me. You should have trusted me. My nefarious plan was all inside your suspicious little head. I never made it, never mind executed it."

"I had no way of knowing that at the time."

"You could have trusted me. That's what wives do with their husbands."

"We never got married."

"Your decision, not mine."

They stared at each other for a long moment.

"What do you want me to do?" she finally asked, then quickly added, "About Kayla and Matt's wedding?"

"Don't worry. I know you'd never ask what I wanted you to do about us."

His words brought a pain to Angelica's stomach. He was up there on his pedestal of self-righteous anger, and she was down here…missing him.

Don't miss
REUNITED WITH THE LASSITER BRIDE
by Barbara Dunlop.

Available September 2014 wherever
Harlequin® Desire books and ebooks are sold.